A RING
AROUND THE
MOON

A Ring Around The Moon

by

Dave Thelwell

Central Publishing Limited
West Yorkshire

Paperback ISBN 1 903970 06 7

Published
by

Central Publishing Limited
Rotd Street Offices
Milnsbridge
Huddersfield
West Yorkshire
HD3 4QY

www.centralpublishing.co.uk

DEDICATION

I would like to dedicate this book to my father, whose stories of his own life growing up and working on the land have inspired so many characters within these pages. And even now, in his eighties, he still has the ability to make people laugh at his antics.

Thanks Dad.

PREFACE

Christmas was over and done with, and the villagers were looking onwards with anticipation to the start of nineteen sixty-seven, only a few days away. Plans for the celebration of the New Year were already being discussed in The Bowlers Arms, the local drinking establishment, where some intoxicated late-night drinkers were mulling over their last dregs of beer and the idea of a fancy dress party.

Nineteen sixty-six had been a good year, and although sorry to see its departure, the good folk were casting their minds forward to the forthcoming twelve months and the prospects that lay ahead.

The village of Barnsford lay in the rolling countryside of the shires, exactly halfway between the city of Chesham to the north and the market town of Whiteworth to the south, in the county of Warmingshire. It was a green and yellow patchwork of fields and woods in the spring and summer, an ever-changing kaleidoscope of golds and browns in the autumn and wintertime.

It was the epitome of rural England: farms, village school, small shops, pretty little cottages, the parish church with its tall and domineering tower, and Barnsford Hall, home to Squire

Barnsford, employer to many, landlord to most.

Although life was led at a leisurely pace, it wasn't without its moments, and the pages that unfold will give the reader an insight into the lives of the inhabitants of a country village in the mid nineteen hundreds. When farms were places that catered for the feeding of the masses, when cows had names like Daisy, Marigold and Buttercup, when children would find employment and homes within their own community upon leaving school. When a little scullery doubled up as a Post Office, and allowed a little old lady a chance to earn some extra coppers to supplement her pension by handing out pensions to others. When it didn't matter how many or how few attended the village school, it would always be there to educate and teach the young right and wrong. When everyone in the parish knew everyone else, when people lived in harmony with the fauna and flora they shared the countryside with, and when a man could tuck his shirt into his underpants without the fear of being improperly dressed.

Barnsford would soon be forced, kicking and screaming, to catch up with the rest of the world, but at the dawn of nineteen sixty seven, it just sauntered along, taking each day as it came, and trying the best that it could to keep its own house in order.

A Ring Around The Moon

...just where Nancy's buttocks were almost forcing them to tearing point, were two black hand-prints, identical in size to that of the landlord's...

CHAPTER ONE

BETTER THE DEVIL YOU KNOW

Jack Frost had risen, dressed, and been out and about for hours, covering the countryside in a veil of crispy whiteness. The residue of Christmas snowfall had now changed from the powdery icing sugar, that had fallen from the sky on Christmas Eve like goose down, into great lumps of ice. Eric Cartright looked at the needle of the barometer as it moved about the brass face of the battered old instrument hanging on the wall of his cluttered-up hallway. His weather forecasting now depended entirely upon the aches and pains his body had to endure, and he boldly declared to Miss Parkinson, a newcomer to the village, that it would take at least another fall of snow to shift the dirty brown mud-splattered drifts that now remained.

Nevertheless, regardless of the Arctic conditions which now held the village and surrounding areas in their relentless grasp, a ball of bright orange was beginning to ascend into a cloudless blue sky from behind Bickerty Hill, its reflection glistening from the windows of Squire Barnsford's Ice Palace as though they were decorations on a Christmas cake.

Despite everywhere having taken on this impression of a scene from some magical wintry fairy tale, somehow the village of Barnsford didn't appear at all as it ought to have been, especially at nine o'clock on a weekday morning.

Where was everyone? Why wasn't the paper shop open, enabling Harry Gittins' stalwart band of paper lads to deliver the morning's news?

Why was no one waiting for the nine o'clock bus? Why, hours after closing time, were the outside lights of The Bowlers Arms still in full blaze? What reason was there for the back end of Peter Stewart's motorbike to be sticking out of Frank Hanley's privet hedge? Above all, what was Police Constable Doug Billbrock's Morris Minor patrol car doing, submerged in the middle of the village pond with only the top of the roof and the police sign protruding out of the thick ice that covered the water?

To answer these questions we need to return to the night after Boxing Day the previous week, when, after closing time, a rather drunken band of The Bowlers' more regular customers were discussing plans with their hosts, John Wilson and his wife Doreen, about organizing a fancy dress party for New Year's Eve.

It had been the brainchild of Harry Gittins, who'd been told by one of his customers that the Red Lion at Tilbury was entertaining the idea. But by now, the plans for the organisation of this, the first of Barnsford's social dates for 1967 (or was it the last for 1966? After four hours' deliberation they still couldn't quite decide) had been taken over by a rather enthusiastic and completely inebriated Major Bantam.

"What about a theme?" the Major slurred, remembering the glamorous balls held in the officers' mess when he was in service; but, in doing so, failing to picture the likes of Gus Devenport - a local farmer with a taste for the sweet things in life - and his twenty-eight stone figure squeezed into a Harlequin outfit.

"Not a lot of time for everyone to prepare fer sumit like that," Harry said; who, having seen pictures of some of the bright young things the Major was fashioning in his mind's eye, in the Country Life magazine he sold in his shop, had somehow managed to get his imagination around the though of Gus's portly frame wedged into a Harlequin outfit.

"Best if thee lets 'em come as owt, gives 'em more scope like," he suggested, trying not to hurt the Major's feelings.

John and Doreen, who were still marvelling at the Christmas takings, had been quick to give their blessing to the plan, thinking that this was another sure-fire earner. So, by the next day, the hand-made posters that the Major had risen early the following morning to produce in his study were distributed around the village, where they hung in all the shops, village hall, post office, and, of course, The Bowlers Arms, venue of the event.

Everyone in the village greeted the idea with the same enthusiasm that they had brought to the planning of the floats for the village fete. They set about making their plans for a costume that would hopefully win the five pounds prize money that John Wilson had so generously donated for the best and most original idea.

Peter Stewart, the village handyman, had decided on a cowboy as his theme - something that many, having been the victims of Peter's somewhat bodged attempts at plumbing or electrical work, thought a little ironic. So, dressed in the checked shirt and blue jeans he wore for work every single day, he made his character come to life with a kiss-me-quick cowboy hat and a pair of toy guns wedged into star-studded holsters which he had borrowed from his young nephew Billy; who, being the little entrepreneur he was, had insisted on a down-payment of sixpence and a shilling a day rent.

Eric Cartright, the village builder, turned up dressed as a pirate, complete with hooped tee shirt. Which, due to the beer-belly he proudly boasted that he'd paid a lot of money for, made some think he'd come as the planet Saturn. Masked in a spotted headscarf, a curtain ring tied around his ear with a piece of cotton, he completed the guise with a trusty plastic cutlass tucked into his thick leather belt. Having found a tableful of women at which to abandon his wife, he wandered over to the bar and proceeded to try and consume as much liquid as made up the entire seven seas.

Everyone congratulated Gus Devenport on his attempt to emulate a marrow, only to realise by his look of total bewilderment, that, having not been in the village since Boxing Day, he hadn't even known about the fancy dress, and was, in fact, wearing the new suit his wife had tailored herself for him to wear at his nephew's wedding the previous Spring. It was made of the finest chair covering material Chesham's number one haberdashery, Mountfords and Sons, could supply; a deep green material, with a fine yellow stripe running from top to bottom. The rest of the wedding party had commented politely amongst themselves that the jovial farmer looked like a walking display from the harvest festival, with Gus's bright red cheeks looking like two ripe tomatoes, his blonde curly hair giving the impression of a cauliflower, and the two highly polished brown work boots that he wore for special occasions peeping out from under the huge turn ups of his trousers like a pair of King Edward potatoes.

Mr Hermit, the primary school teacher, arrived as the pantomime dame that he was portraying the following week in the village amateur dramatic society's production of Aladdin, hoping that his effort would not only earn him the landlord's reward, but would also give the composition a little publicity. In fact, the attention he attracted was far more unwanted, having his bum tweaked no fewer than six times by some of the older farmers of the community, whose failing eyesight must have made them mistake him for one of John Wilson's new barmaids. But after an offer from Wilf Jones the local poacher (who'd never been blessed with the qualities to attract women) to walk him home at the end of the evening, he decided it best to slip quietly away to see the New Year in listening to his collection of Gilbert and Sullivan records in the confines of his own home.

Wilf Jones himself had actually come as a poacher; wearing nets, snares, and the other tools of his illegal pastime around his blood-stained belt, as he revelled in the opportunity of rubbing the noses of those who spent the rest of the year trying to catch him at his pursuits; as well as turning the noses away of those unfortunate enough to be sitting near him.

There were four more cowboys, two Red Indians, half a dozen policemen, an Arab Sheik, milk maids, witches, scarecrows, and various attempts at impersonating the TV characters they watched on their screens each week, filling the pub with what could only be likened to the canteen of a Hollywood studio, or that of a psychiatrist's waiting room.

John Wilson, having put on the new trendy shirt (the purple one with the white collar that Doreen had bought him as a Christmas present) the wrong way round, a black jacket, and wearing a large crucifix that he'd cut out of the gold paper from around a chocolate bar, looked just the part, and would easily have passed as a man of the cloth had he been standing in the pulpit of Barnsford Church on a Sunday morning.

Doreen, never being one to improvise, had driven into Chesham the previous day to visit the theatrical shop in the High Street. Smitten by the shear vividness of the deep red cloth, she hired a Devil's outfit, complete with a three-pronged fork.

To complete the bar staff's masquerades, Nancy Baily, who was famous in the village for her short skirts, shapely legs, perfectly rounded bottom, rather large breasts, and flirtatious ways with the customers, blackened her face with the theatrical paint. With a bat of her large false eyelashes she'd had Major Bantam, who ran the village theatrical society, scurry home for it the previous night. With the aid of a black curly wig she'd borrowed from her sister, a short blue jacket, a yellow waistcoat, red bell-bottom trousers, a blue and white striped shirt, and a red bow tie, she had turned herself into the most beautiful Golliwog one could ever hope to meet outside of a child's nursery. This completed the most memorable trio of pint-pullers that had ever served The Bowlers' normally dowdy clientele.

As it turned out, it was this combination of Vicar, Devil and Golliwog that was to be the cause of that night's excitement and the following morning's scene of chaos within the village.

The evening started splendidly, with most of the regulars taking part with the usual zest they showed for such occasions. So much so, that by two in the morning, long after the exuberant choruses of Auld Lang Syne and the Hokey Kokey had been sung, they'd all consumed so much ale that John Wilson had to send Nancy down to change the barrel of bitter again.

After a time struggling on her own, Nancy called up from the cellar, in her usual provocative way, for John to give her a hand. John, seeing that Doreen was coping splendidly with the remaining customers, and therefore had her attention well and truly occupied, went down to her assistance two steps at a time in the hope of a quick grope and a kiss while Nancy was still feeling charitable enough to let him.

No one really knows what went on down there, but after enough time to change half a dozen barrels, John and Nancy returned to resume their posts behind the bar as if it had been a matter of routine.

"There, that's that done," John slurred in the same manner as most of his customers were now doing, having consumed his own fair share of the night's supplies. But, looking across at her husband, Doreen didn't seem at all impressed at his show of gallantry. The colour in her normally pale face began to take on the same vivid shade of red as her Devil's outfit as she glared at John through her fiery eyes.

It was then that John realised the reason for this hostile countenance. Behind his furious wife, in the reflection from the bar mirror, John could make out the black smudges that covered his face as if he'd just completed a day down a coal mine, and, looking down at the palms of his hands, he could see the same blackness on them too.

Following his wife's gaze in the direction of Nancy's posterior, there, on the red fabric of the bell-bottom trousers, just where Nancy's buttocks were almost forcing them to tearing point, were two black hand-prints, identical in size to that of the landlord's – Nancy's boss and Doreen's husband.

"You, you dirty old bugger," Doreen screamed at her spouse, causing him to wonder whether she was on about his uncleanliness, or the fact it was obvious to her that his philandering ways with the staff had been discovered.

A hush ran through the bar as the remaining customers turned their heads in the direction of their hosts, just in time to witness Doreen pick up the nearest glass. It was Eric Cartright's own personal pint pot, the one with the naked lady on the side that he'd bought on a day out to the seaside over ten years ago. With all the venom of a woman scorned, Doreen hurled it at her husband with the strength of a shot putter.

John, managing to duck in time, waited for the object to go whistling past his head before trying to make a desperate grab for his wife, hopefully in

10

order to calm her down. But, despite being equally as inebriated as he was, she managed a quick side-step to the right, sending John crashing into the optics that hung from the shelf behind her.

Doreen, unconcerned about her semiconscious husband who now lay on the floor with blood gushing from the cut on his forehead, then turned her attention to Nancy Baily.

"I'll give yer Golliwog! When I gets me 'ands on yer, I'll bloody marmalize yer," and with that she lurched forward with every intention of extracting her revenge on the young barmaid.

It was at this point that Nancy thought she would forgo her wages for once and try and leave with her life intact. Throwing up the hatch of the bar, hitting Eric Cartright on the side of the head as she did so and causing him to pass out at the bar for the first time in twelve years, Nancy flew through the door into the street and off in the direction of the church, probably hoping to find sanctuary from the Devil and damnations that were following her. Doreen, stepping over the body of a comatose Eric, gave chase, and, for a woman twice the age of her quarry, was closing the gap at an incredible rate.

John pulled himself to his feet; grabbing at a bar towel, he held it to his gashed forehead in the hope of curtailing the flow of blood. He raced out after the two women, followed very closely by a witch, two policemen, Major Bantam (organiser of the evening's revelry), and something resembling a marrow.

By the time they'd got half way down the street, Doreen had caught hold of Nancy, and was now on her back hitting her over the head with an ashtray bearing an advertisement for the hospitality of an Allington's Brewery Inn, which she'd snatched up off one of the tables as she'd left.

Catching up with them, John, gasping for breath after the run from the pub - the only exercise he'd taken in the last twenty years or so - tried to drag his wife off. But Doreen, spitting out her words of hate as if she was possessed by the very same Devil she'd been trying to impersonate, was clinging on like a limpet, and continuing to bash her adversary to death with the ashtray.

While all this was going on, approaching the village from the direction of Chesham was Doug Billbrook, constable of the parish. He happened to be doing his late night rounds with Sergeant Mills, head of this rural beat and normally stationed at the area headquarters at Tilbury. Having spotted Peter Stewart dressed as a cowboy leaving the pub car park on his motorcycle, he began to follow in order to inquire if he'd been drinking; which, Doug knew, was going to be like asking a woman leaving a department store if she'd been shopping.

Travelling in the opposite direction, from Whiteworth on her way back from attending her second birth of the night, was Miss Prim, midwife of the district. As her name intimated, she had lived her life trying to avoid the unseemly things that went on around her, and always wondered how people could enter into the improper act that made her job possible.

As she entered the village, driving as cautiously as she possibly could on the treacherous icy road, she once more rubbed the windscreen in order to remove the ice that was forming on it from her cold breath.

Peering through the hole she'd made, and knowing nothing at all about the fancy dress party at the Bowlers, she suddenly found herself witnessing the most bizarre scene of her sheltered life.

There, on the grass verge alongside the church wall, was the Devil attacking a golliwog with an ashtray; and the Devil, if it hadn't been for the vicar, who was covered in blood and trying the best he could to pull this Satanic figure off, would soon be forcing the life-sized child's doll through the surface of the earth, and down into the bowels of Hell itself.

Standing round these ghoulish goings-on, were: policemen, Red Indians, pirates, witches, and something resembling a prize-winning marrow with legs. Although her instincts told her to get out of there as fast as she could, fear had caused her fingers to lock tight on the steering wheel, inducing her to head straight for this unholy group.

If it hadn't been for the fact that everyone suddenly turned to face her, screaming in the same manner that she had begun to, then she probably

13

would never have come to her senses. But, luckily for them, she did; and, swerving away from these macabre goings on, she came face to face with a cowboy straddled on what looked like a headless steed.

Peter Stewart swerved to avoid being hit, only to ride straight into Frank Hanley's privet hedge on the other side of the road. Miss Prim's car carried on, her eyes now locked upon the ghostly rodeo rider, as it disappeared into the scrub.

Doug Billbrook had to take immediate action to prevent what could have been a head-on collision. Veering off the road, the police car skated across the ice-covered pond until it came to rest right in the middle.

Just as the two officers of the law had made their exits, and despite the three-inch thick ice which had been strong enough to hold Barnsford's equivalent of the winter Olympics on for the last week, there was a great cracking sound, and the vehicle suddenly dropped about four feet, leaving only the roof and police sign visible.

Maybe, and only maybe, everyone would have got off with a warning, but for the fact that Eric Cartright, having come round from his clout over the head from the bar hatch, wandered outside to see where everyone had gone. He took one look at the sergeant and, believing him to be the one who'd cracked him over the head, (and also mistaking him for the policeman seen giving his long-suffering wife a kiss in the bar when he'd still been too sober to care) hit the sergeant smack in the mouth with a punch that would have felled an ox.

Sergeant Mills, with blood pouring from his cut and swollen lip, made a call from the local phone box, while lisping through two loose teeth. This allowed John Wilson enough time to lock The Bowlers' front door, before the Black Maria arrived and the members of the fancy dress party were loaded up and taken to the police station at Chesham. From whence, having spent the night sobering up, they were all allowed to make their own way home, (with just a caution to their credit) the following morning.

At first, Bill thought it was amusing when the lad kept coming to him to ask for a long weight or a left-handed screwdriver.

CHAPTER TWO

THE PLUMBER'S APPRENTICE

It took the village a while to recover from the embarrassment of New Year's Eve. Those who'd been involved on that calamitous night, couldn't even bring themselves to discuss it, although those who'd been wise enough to go home when they'd had their fill made up for the others' silence. Despite it being common knowledge as to who'd been implicated, this didn't stop them from asking, each time they bumped into one of the guilty party:

"Did thee hear what went on at the Bowlers t'other nit after we left? Shocking, wasn't it?"

Which always met with a swallow, a splutter, a shake of the head, and a look of complete surprise when informed of the disgraceful behaviour of those members of the community less disciplined than the orator.

To the great relief of the customers, by the end of January, John and Doreen had once again started communicating with one another. Although it was only in the way of a sharp command, teamed with an equally biting reply, it was at least better than the silence everyone had been made to endure since that dreaded night.

Nancy, as you can imagine, never returned, finding herself another post behind the bar at the Red Lion of Tilbury, and although she took a few of the more lecherous Bowlers' clients with her, she was soon deserted for the 'better bitter' that the Bowlers served up.

Taking no chances, Doreen replaced her with a fifty-six year old, fifteen stone, buxom serving wench named Meg Green; and, although not having quite the same pulling power with the men that Nancy had, she made up for it with her attractive nature, and the way she could pull the perfect pint. But, despite chastising anyone who irritated her with language that would have made Eric Cartright blush, she soon became the pin-up of everyone who enjoyed a good pint and a bit of a laugh whilst they were out.

Winter continued to embrace the village in its less than hospitable bosom, causing havoc in the way of frozen and burst pipes. This, of course, meant extra work for Bill Dutton, the estate plumber. So much so, that Lord Barnsford's new clerk of works, Dennis Gough (a wet-behind-the-ears young man from Chesham; who, despite having all the right letters to follow his name, never looked like coming to terms with the hands-on experiences he was now getting) decided, in his wisdom, to hire a young lad for the post of apprentice to Bill.

Martin Speers wasn't so much a bad apprentice as accident-prone. The lad was keen enough, even a good worker when left on his own with a simple task to do. But to Bill, it was as if Dennis Gough had chosen Lucifer himself to aid him in what was now becoming an over-stretched work load. This, of course, was something that neither Bill, nor any other member of the estate workforce, had ever been used to.

Within the first week, young Martin had thrown his cigarette out of the Mini pickup window as they sped towards yet another flooded kitchen, accidentally setting alight the hessian sacking that Bill used to lag the pipes and tanks (hence turning the back of the vehicle into a blazing inferno), and ricked Bill's back as they attempted to haul an old bath down a difficult winding stairway, thus giving the old bugger the perfect excuse the following day for his defeat in the village snooker contest. He also dropped a lump hammer clean through the bottom of a brand new lavatory that had just been installed with much effort and great skill by his mentor.

At first, Bill thought it was amusing when the lad kept coming to him to ask for a long weight or a left-handed screwdriver. But it didn't take long for that amusement to turn to annoyance, especially when, after a great deal of struggling to get there, he was just making himself comfortable in some tiny corner of an attic, up would pop the lad's head through the hatch.

"Bill, where's the elbow grease?"

"Bill, where's the spare bubble for the level?"

"Bill, where's the glass hammer?"

After cottoning on to the fact that every time the lad was asked to go on some ridiculous mission by other members of the estate workforce, and always doing it with zest and smelling of cigarettes on his return, Bill decided it was time to ban him from running errands for any of the men - other than himself.

Bill made a point of letting the lad and the rest of the gang know that, from then on, he would only be allowed to go for articles that Bill himself had sent him for. Which, once again to Bill's annoyance, nearly always turned out to be the wrong item retrieved.

Things came to a head when one morning, not long after arriving at the yard and having not yet made himself a cup of tea, the phone rang with a request for the plumber to be urgently sent around to the Bowlers Arms. Apparently, water was dripping into the main bar, via John and Doreen's bedroom, from the tank room situated above.

Packing the various bits and pieces he was likely to need to rectify the problem, Bill popped his head back into the mess room and summoned Martin with a scowl.

"Come on, lad, we anner got all day. I wants t' be back here in time fer break."

"Coming, Bill," the lad stammered, dreading yet another day of the bad tempered old bugger's bawling and shouting. "Con I just finish me tea?"

"Finish yer tea! I anner even 'ad chance t'bloody well 'ave one. No, yer bloody well conner," and with that he marched across to the makeshift table the men were sitting around, reached across, and clipped the lad around his ear. This caused more embarrassment to Martin than actual pain, but nevertheless, due to the extreme cold, set his ear glowing like metal in a blacksmith's forge within seconds of the blow landing.

"The lad's in fer it t'day. Bill's in a wos mood than ever," Bob Black the joiner commented, as he gazed through the grimy window at the plumber and his apprentice climbing into the pickup.

"Yes. I think it's a damn shame, the way he treats that boy. Anyone would think he'd never been young and green himself," commented Tarquin Jones. Tarquin was a good-tempered sort, born in the heart of Wales and very well educated for an estate worker. Although he never liked to interfere with the teaching of the apprentices, he'd never liked the way that Bill had treated Martin since the day the lad had first begun working there.

Arriving at the Bowlers, Bill and Martin were met by a rather frantic Doreen Wilson.

"Hurry up lads, it's going t' ruin me bloody carpets if yer dunner stop it soon."

"Dunner werrit, Doreen, we'll soon have it under control," Bill assured her, turning around and shouting at young Martin, "Dunner just sit

21

there lad, git the gear off the van and bring it in!" making his way himself into the pub empty-handed.

"'Ave yer turned off the stopcock?" Bill enquired of the landlady.

"No. I dunner know where it is," she sheepishly admitted, feeling rather foolish about the fact that she'd never even given it a thought.

Being familiar with the waterworks of the Bowlers Arms, Bill headed straight through the pub and into the scullery where, within seconds he'd turned off the main stopcock; something that would have spared them the pool of water that had now formed in the middle of the bar floor if Doreen had done it.

Clambering awkwardly into the loft through the small hatch at the top of the stairs, Bill gave young Martin instructions to hand him up his tools, and then sarcastically asked, if 'it weren't too much trouble', could he see if he could git a mop and bucket and start cleaning up the floor down below.

Martin proceeded, as he always tried to do, to get on with what task Bill had set him, with the intention of pleasing the miserable old bugger, and earn himself some Brownie points. It was while he was busy doing this that Bill hollered from out of the attic for him to fetch him some solder; which, due to the muffling of the attic lagging and the echoing of the hall and stairs, sounded to the poor lad like, 'turn on the water!' Being too frightened to query the order in case it met with the usual:

"Are yer bloody deaf, lad?" found the incoming main and turned the stopcock fully open.

The water rushed through the system with the urgency of a bullet from a gun, finding, in only a matter of seconds, the neatly axe-sawed piece of pipe that Bill was just about to put a coupling on.

"That's if," Bill muttered quietly under his breath, "that damn' lad would hurry up with the solder."

Whoosh! The full force of freezing cold water hit the plumber smack in the face, sending him reeling backwards, and soaking him from head to toe.

Spluttering and gasping, Bill turned to the loft hatch, and shoving his head through it, gazed down the stairway in disbelief at Martin standing at the bottom with a rather pleased smile of satisfaction spread across his face - as though he'd just done something to be proud of.

"You bloody great fool! What the bloody hell der yer think tha's playing at?" Bill yelled with venom. Then, just as he was about to hurl even more abuse at the lad, his teeth (which never had been a great fit) dropped out of his mouth and, upon hitting the landing floor, proceeded to bounce all the way down the steep staircase, through the door at the bottom, and into the bar.

Now unfortunately for Bill, it just happened that it had turned eleven o'clock, and also, more unfortunately, due to the fact that it was too bloody cold to do any work on the farm, the twenty-eight stone Gus Devenport had just popped in for a dinner time session.

The dentures, which by now had already suffered a few loosened molars, rolled just under where Gus's sized twelve boots (which were covered in the best fertilizer available to man - cow shit) were landing with a soft thud upon the floor. Crack! The tea-stained teeth were shattered as the entire weight of this huge farmer came to rest.

Martin, finally able to understand the gummy retorts coming from Bill's mouth, dashed back into the kitchen and turned the stopcock off again. Unfortunately not before the build-up of water had finally caused the ceiling to collapse, and come crashing down on John and Doreen's bed, covering the two-hundred-year-old four poster with a brown and smelly deluge from the old rusty pipes that carried the supply to all the taps in the pub.

Gus, wondering what had caused the crunching noise from beneath his feet, lifted his enormous foundations upwards and, stooping down, picked up the fragmented remains of what had once been Bill Dutton's rather too seldom-seen smile.

Despite the damage done that day, Martin avoided getting the sack by the skin of his own white pearlies, and continued in the post of whipping-boy to Bill for the rest of his apprenticeship. After a further three years in the employment of the Squire, he went on to start up his own plumbing business in Chesham, and a damn fine one it turned out to be, thanks to the strict, although mostly happy, time that he'd spent under Bill's somewhat demanding regime.

In fact, once out of his apprenticeship, the two became the best of friends, and it was a rather sad Bill Dutton who made a touching speech and wished young Martin all the best (at The Bowlers on the day of his leaving presentation). He was presented with a new watch, bought with great pride with money donated by the rest of the gang. As an extra memento of the time spent on the Barnsford Estate, he was given the disintegrated remnants of Bill's teeth (which John Wilson had put away for safe-keeping in a place where they'd remained, totally forgotten, until the previous week. When being told of the presentation, he remembered all about them and exactly where they were). Along with them was a tube of glue, and the instructions that, if he ever had a slack period from the every day hustle and bustle, of what was now referred to as a 'central heating engineer', he could perhaps have a go at repairing them as a spare set for his old sparring partner.

...*Gus and Mildred, to everyone's amazement, were brilliant, gliding round the floor as though they were on a carpet of air.*

CHAPTER THREE

LEAD THE MERRY DANCE

Major Bantam, having just finished viewing 'Come Dancing' on the television, and reminiscing with his good lady wife about the times he and she had twirled the evenings away in the officers' mess, decided it would be a good idea to put his stepping ability (along with his expertise at motivating the masses), into organising a dance school in the village hall. With the aid of Margaret (Mrs Bantam), they could once again re-live the glory of those medal-winning years.

The Major had been a model soldier and officer for over thirty years, serving his country with the gallantry expected of the leading classes. Now, in his retirement, with an army pension to sustain him, plus the money left to him on the death of his father, The Right Honourable Sir Anthony Bantam (Chesham's Member of Parliament for twenty six years), the good Major had decided to spend his remaining days organising the residents of Barnsford into activities of varying kinds.

He'd been the one to start the badminton club, whose members met every Monday evening in the village hall, and thrashed a poor defenceless shuttlecock back and forth across the room as if it were a wasp about to land in their drink.

When the Woman's Institute had decided to produce their own pantomime (in competition with the one that Tilbury, the neighbouring village held each year), who was the ladies' first choice as director? Major Bantam.

President of the bowls club, chairman of the cricket club, captain of the tennis club, and secretary of the Barnsford fête committee, were among just some of the more prominent positions he held. Along with each post came the enthusiasm for the job of a man who was trying to climb his way to the top in life, not seeing out his retirement and enjoying the peace and rest that most men would have been glad of.

The posters, that he and Margaret had manufactured together on pink paper (Margaret's idea), and in true military style (the Major's), proclaimed the starting of a ballroom dance class, by Jeremy and Margaret Bantam. To show the less knowledgeable members of the community what to expect, Camilla (the Major's daughter), had sketched a couple, not surprisingly resembling the Major and his wife in their younger days, swirling about a dance floor in full regalia.

These were distributed around the village, being displayed in all the prominent places: Harry Gittins' newsagents, Arthur Blake's emporium (proprietor of the 'Get It All' grocery establishment), Tom Stanworth's butchers, the village hall itself (the venue of the dance school), the church notice board, the village notice board, and, probably where it would receive the most notice, in the bar of The Bowlers Arms. Where, although being the source of much amusement amongst the men folk, it was read with a great deal of interest by their good ladies. Who persuasively informed their spouses on the way home that, in the interest of marital bliss, they would be expected to be their partners when the lessons began the following Monday evening. This would be seven-thirty sharp, for the price of two shillings and sixpence a session, a cup of tea and biscuit inclusive.

Tea time, on the night of the big occasion, brought about more moaning and excuses, as to why each husband could not attend, than their offspring had made earlier that day as to why they ought to remain at home and not attend school.

"Bloody hell, woman, 'ave bin sloggin mesen t' death all day in the bloody fields. Last thing I wanner be doin' now is prattin' about like a bloody jessy in the village hall," Jim Broadlever, one of the Home farm workforce, protested.

"I'd love t' tak thee, but I think I've ricked me back liftin' some brick t'day," Eric Cartwright informed his wife, in the hope that the thought of her poor husband trying to dance with a bad back would bring about sympathy and understanding. Of course, he would make a miraculous recovery about nine o'clock and be allowed to make it to the Bowlers for the last hour and a half.

"Bloody cow looks like calvin, t'nit, an I was lookin forard t' takin thee t' dance an' all."

"I'm expectin' a call from customer, about a big order."

"Car's bin playin' up, a' dunner trust it t' tak us in t' village till I git her fixed."

"Me goin-out shoes are knackered."

"I heard in newsagents th's afternoon, that the dance classes 'ave bin called off, due t' Major 'avin broockin his leg."

But, despite the excuses which ranged from tiredness, through to downright lies spreading through the village like a plague, the turn-out for the first ever meeting of the Jeremy and Margaret Bantam dance classes was as well attended as New Year's Eve in the Bowlers. This, much to John Wilson's disgust, left him alone in his establishment for most of the night. (Well, except for Peter Stewart and Wilf Jones who, being bachelors, had no one to go with, making them the happiest and most envied men in the village.)

They turned up in their various shapes and sizes: tall men with small wives, thin men with fat wives, fat men with fat wives, small men with large wives, fat men with thin wives, and in the case of Mr and Mrs Bower, who resided in the nine houses, where the small doorways and beamed ceilings were a handicap to both of them, very tall men with very tall wives.

Some had danced before and this, although their repertoire consisted of only the social fox trot, waltz and twist, made them feel vastly superior to those whose knowledge of tripping the light fantastic was a quick Hokey Kokey on New Year's Eve.

Major Bantam did the best he could to place them in groups without making his scholars' feel in the slightest bit inferior to each other, and then, ascertaining who could do what with whom, with the aid of his portable record player and collection of ballroom dance records, proceeded to get the classes under way.

By the end of the first night, the village hall resembled the physiotherapy ward of Chesham General. Corns had been trodden on, shins had been kicked, backs had been strained, muscles pulled, and varicose veins ached. With all this, and the many arguments between the spouses as to who was doing what wrongly, it was surprising that any of the couples were talking to each other the following week.

By the second week the numbers had halved. The third week had seen them quartered. After only one month, the Major and his wife were left with only four couples. By the time the refreshments had been paid for, the revenue from these stalwart Terpsichoreans hardly covered the hire of the hall.

Still the Major wasn't put off, his intentions never having been to make a profit from the exercise, but to educate the people as to the refinements of a civilised society and bring back a few happy memories of his own. So, every Monday, with the exception of Bank Holidays and illness, these eight students would be put through their paces as if on parade, with the promise that when the Major thought them ready, he would put them up for their bronze medals. Seeing he was certain that no one would fail (due to the fact that the test took as long as it needed to get it right), they would celebrate the presentation of their honours at a dance held in the hall, with a band and invitations to all around to attend.

So in the search for perfection, lessons were taken so seriously that the idea they were doing it for fun had completely gone from their intent. Black looks, snide remarks, petty quarrels, and sometimes complete walk-outs happened, with such regularity that it was hard to see what they saw in this weekly pursuit.

And yet each week they put so much concentration in to perfecting their steps that grown men, men who'd known how to drink, fight and swear; men who could spit, belch and fart as good as any other, could be seen twirling about the floor with the Major's one hand placed firmly upon their shoulder and the other around their waist. Despite the Major's insistence that they held him tightly around his waist, they hung on reluctantly as if he'd just broken wind after one of the Squire's banquets.

They were watched closely by their wives, who,

relieved that it wasn't them that had got it wrong, stood on the side lines trying not to laugh at the thought of what their drinking pals would say if they ever found out. They wished that right now they had a Kodak Brownie in their possession, so they'd have some leverage when it came to the occasion when a room needed decorating, or an item for the house needed replacing.

According to their ability to learn, their dexterity, and their co-ordination, each couple reached a certain standard in the waltz, foxtrot, quickstep, samba, cha-cha-cha, tango and jive, learning how to dip, toe and heel and twirl in a fashion that gave them the satisfaction of knowing their hard work was beginning to pay off.

They practised and tried to perfect their various moves back home, with the hope that, by the following week, they would sparkle in the eyes of the Major, who would praise them with cries of "Splendid!" "Well done, that man!" "I say, just like Fred and Ginger."

Or, if they failed to reach the standards expected, would be chastised with remarks like: "Hold your head up." "Come, come now, stomachs in, chests out." "On your toes, Arthur, on your toes." Making them each in turn, feel like children being scolded in front of the entire class.

The exams were held on a Saturday morning, meaning that a good many had to find an excuse for asking for time off work; or, in the case of a couple of farmers, make sure their hired hands were left with plenty to do in their absence.

They all waited in the kitchen of the village hall, as in turn the couples entered the hall itself, and performed in front of the Major and Mr Harold Pikes, the examiner from the local branch of the 'Association of British Ballroom Dancing.'

Mr Pike stood solemn-faced as they twirled, tripped, spun, staggered, stepped, and slipped their way round, as though they were performing on a floor made of chewing gum and ice. Occasionally, he could be caught making notes on his pad where, it has to be said, the pen slipped across the paper with a great deal more elegance than his examinees were doing on the dance floor!

At the end of the morning, everyone had been seen, tried and tested. So, administering his best wishes to the Major, and with a rather sympathetic handshake and a tap on the shoulder, Mr Pike bade him goodbye with the promise that he'd let him have the results of the test as soon as possible. With that, he climbed into his little M.G. sports car, and made his way out of the village, back on the road to the civilisation and cultural surroundings of the big City. He was thinking to himself that, although all of them would receive their certificates and medals at a cost of two pounds, two shillings and sixpence each, the world of ballroom dancing would be a great deal better off if the quaint folk of Barnsford would stick to jigging about amongst bales of hay at their local barn dances.

The big night arrived and the village hall looked like a scene from a Hollywood film set. The light that usually hung from the centre rafter had been taken down and replaced with a huge shimmering, glittering sphere. Flowers adorned every nook and cranny. The tables had been set as though it was the 'Ritz', and the Major and his good lady stood at the door, greeting the guests as they arrived, dressed as if they were in fact awaiting the arrival of Heads of State of all the Countries in the Commonwealth.

The Major cut a dashing figure in his red army tunic, decorated with so many ribbons and medals that it left his neighbours in awe as to what a heroic figure he must have been. To add to the uniform, he also wore his black trousers with the yellow stripes which ran up either side of his legs; a cummerbund; shoes that you could see your face in; and a white starched shirt that looked as though it would decapitate his head should he make any sudden move to look down.

Margaret wore a stunning blue ball gown teamed with gold dance shoes, which had heels that were so high they gave her the appearance of being just about to topple forward onto the guests as each in turn shook her hand and congratulated her on her appearance.

As well as the proud recipients of the night's awards, the Major had invited just about everyone he knew, from the rough and ready members of the community, to friends in high places. And although a little worried by the social gap that separated these differing classes, the Major was far too concerned that everything should go to plan, so that the thought of Mr and Mrs Barker-Trumpter (proprietors of Warmingly Grange, watering hole of the country set), mingling with Eric Cartright at the bar had never really crossed his mind. Having just congratulated His Nibs on what a nice establishment they had, Eric went on to advise him 'that it would be a lot better', and would receive more visits from Eric and his cronies, if they got in draught Warburtons, 'instead of the shit he tried to pass off as beer'.

The only member of the ruling classes who didn't attend was the Squire himself; who, trying to protect the community from the wrath of Lady Lucy, his wife, very rarely attended anything other than the village fete.

Eric Cartright had once likened Lady Lucy's expression on mingling with the villagers as 'resembling a bulldog, licking piss off a thistle', (which had something to do with the pious expression that never left her face when in the presence of the likes of him). She had a face that gave everyone the impression it had been carved from a lump of granite, and then dropped from the top of Barnsford church.

It was an expression very rarely seen in public, unless in the company of her ladies at the Women's Institute, a society of which she was the lady Chairperson. Yet, somewhere behind that hard and bitter façade, had once existed the femininity of a beautiful Debutante, who'd been the life and soul of any party, thus causing a young and, considered by many, handsome Squire, to fall madly in love with her.

Yes, it was true; the Squire had loved her at some time in his life. But for as long as most people cared to remember, that feeling had turned to a sense of begrudging responsibility so that, given the chance, he'd have loved to have paid someone to get rid of many a year past.

The dance progressed, with the Upper Crust swishing about, displaying the experience of years of attending hunt balls, one or two of the villagers stepping their way through a social foxtrot as though they themselves were at a ball, and the members of the dance class moving about as though they were on casters, running over each other's feet as they sang their own words to the music: "One together, two together, side together, turn".

Sitting in the far corner, taking up the entire room at a table for six, dressed in the green and yellow suit his wife had fabricated for him, was Gus Devenport, and by his side, or as near to his side as she could get, garbed in what could only be described as a flower-embroidered marquee, was his lady wife, Mildred. Twenty-eight and twenty-seven stone respectively, moving only to allow Gus to get up and make his way to the bar, causing the dancers to alter their course, as he returned each time with two pints of beer. They sat there watching the participants enjoying their evening's cavorting, complimenting the end of each tune and applauding their neighbours as they received their dividends for three months' hard labour.

"Good job old Gus an' his missus inner dancin', the bloody buildin' would collapse!" Den Mullins commented out loud to the rest of the Home Farm men and their spouses, with whom he shared a table.

"Aye, it'd be like an earthquake," Tom Bowen agreed, and although none of them could dance a step themselves, it didn't stop them from enjoying the thought of old Gus battering everyone else out of the way, as he and Mildred steam-rollered their way around the village hall.

As the evening was drawing to an end, and most of the throng had retired to their seats to rub their corns or get their breath back, the Major, who'd been the M. C. for the evening, announced that the band would play a Viennese Waltz. This would give him the chance to show to the community just how good he and his wife had been back then, in the days of their medal-winning years.

The Major and Mrs Bantam held each other as if each were made of china and, along with one or two other couples who thought it wouldn't be beyond their means to perform this elegant number, they waited for the band to prepare themselves to accompany them.

Just as the conductor was about to raise his baton in the air, a loud shuffling and screeching of chairs from the back of the hall interrupted him. Everyone turned round to see what the commotion was, and they all gasped, almost sucking the entire air from the room and creating a vacuum, as Gus and Mildred took up their places upon the floor.

No one spoke; in fact for a few seconds no one breathed, living only on the air they'd managed to store in their lungs. Then, once again composed, the leader of the band gave the signal, and the music began.

The Major and his partner were good. The one or two who'd felt confident enough to put their better upbringing to the test were good. But Gus and Mildred, to everyone's amazement, were brilliant, gliding round the floor as though they were on a carpet of air.

Never once throughout the whole rendition did they put a foot wrong. Shoulders back, heads held high, feet moving with the dexterity of professionals, and, although it was asking the impossible to expect them to have held in their stomachs, they looked as graceful, twirling and whirling about that wooden-boarded village hall floor, as any member of the Austrian aristocracy.

The hall erupted with applause at the end, and Gus took a bow, breaking wind as he did so. Although no one would ever guess that this was the first time they'd ever performed in public, mastering their routine in the confines of the barn back at the farm, the Devenports were as proud as Punch of their execution of this graceful number.

What the rest also knew nothing about was that Mildred, who'd not always been as fat as she was now, had been brought up among the well bred of London. She met Gus at the Royal show where he was displaying his dad's cattle, and she was riding her own horse in the equestrian events, and although being disowned by her parents on their engagement, she had loved this large man enough to give up everything and become a farmer's wife. It was his mam who had taught her to cook, causing her to grow in size as she discovered the pleasures of good old country cooking.

In return for all the instruction on husbandry and horticulture her husband gave her, she taught Gus to dance. Although they'd only ever practised their steps within the farm outbuildings and on a surface covered with straw, watched only by an audience of bullocks and heifers, they turned out to be the stars of the ball.

Albert had always loved the way she kept everything so spotless, and she'd promised him the day he went away that she would never let her standards fall...

CHAPTER FOUR

MOLLY THE MOP

Molly Madley had deserted the warmth of her bed before the crack of dawn, for today was her scheduled day for spring-cleaning. Not that the place was ever allowed to get dirty enough to warrant a spring clean. But every year for the last sixty-two, ever since she'd walked back up the aisle of Barnsford church with Albert, March the first had signalled the start of spring, and that meant putting the new duster she'd purchased from the village shop into action.

Albert, her husband, had long since past away, killed in the trenches of the First World War, but that hadn't stopped Molly from keeping home as though one day he'd come walking back into her life as if he'd never been away.

After climbing into bed that night exhausted by her day's toil, and a little concerned by the pain shed been feeling in her arm all afternoon, she drifted into a deep impenetrable slumber. She quietly thought to herself, as she allowed a blanket of repose to cover her body, that if it were still there tomorrow, she'd pay a visit to Doctor

Killshaw. Although turned sixty himself, he was still referred to by Molly as 't'young doctor', seeing as he was fresh from medical school when first he'd set foot in Barnsford, after taking over from old Doctor Grace on his retirement, and becoming a friend from the day she first went to see him about her piles.

Molly began to dream, returning, as often she did, to her childhood where, with a warm and loving smile upon her mother's face, she was greeted at the front door to their little cottage.

"Molly, I was beginning to fret. It's not like you to be late fer tea."

"I've been picking flowers with Ann Powers in Barley Wood."

She then let out a childish giggle as she held out the beautiful bunch of primroses and violets she'd brought home for her mother.

"Well, come inside and we'll find a vase to put them in. I've made your favourite for tea, bubble and squeak, and bread and butter pudding, so hurry up and wash yer hands. Daddy will be home from the farm soon, and if yer not ready, he'll eat yours as well as his own."

They both giggled now, as the thought of her father's rather healthy appetite caused Molly to quickly remove her wellingtons. Closing the front door behind her, joyfully they made their way up the hall and into the scullery and the sound of their merriment could be heard drifting through the letter box and out into the late afternoon air,

Dave Thelwell

Molly gazed across the room at her father, with his ruddy cheeks, a stomach that had given way to the wonderful cooking her mother had been providing it with for these last ten years, eyes the colour of the reddish brown conkers she picked in the Autumn, and a smile as rich as any Christmas pud.

"Where shall I hang this?" he enquired of Molly, holding aloft a brightly painted wooden soldier he'd made in his little garden shed, along with the other ornaments that were to hang on the Christmas tree.

"Put it just above the snowman that Mummy made," she answered, and running across the room, grabbed her father around the neck and hugged him until he nearly choked.

"This is going to be the best Christmas ever, isn't it, Daddy?" she squealed, and letting go of his neck, planted a big kiss on the side of his cheek.

There were lots of happy Christmases for Molly, but whenever she dreamt, it was always of this one. She was only seven years old, and it snowed. She received from Father Christmas that year the largest dolly she had ever seen. Due to the fact that she had never had any children of her own, it sat, even now, on a chair over at the far side of the bedroom.

"Care t' dance, love?" the young man enquired, and Molly, who'd been taught to dance by her Aunt Jean, but had never been to a harvest supper dance before, couldn't wait to be in the arms of this ever so handsome gallant young swain. With a bit of luck she would be able to put her lessons into practice.

Albert must have danced with her about ten times during the evening, before finally plucking up the courage to ask her out. Although it was only in the way of tea at his mother's house, it seemed to this dizzy nineteen-year-old girl, as though they were dining in some Mediterranean plaza under a scented moonlit sky.

"I do," she replied for the final time to the questions the Reverend Crawley had been asking of her, and on his command, Albert took her in his arms and kissed her. If happiness could be bottled and given to the poor, Molly had enough that day to see that no one need ever want again.

The sun shone as they left the church, the birds seemed to sing louder than Molly had heard them sing before. Albert looked to all the world as though he were a Prince straight out of a Hans Christian Anderson fairy tale.

MISSING IN ACTION. Molly's hand, still clutching the telegram she'd just received, fell limply to her side. She didn't cry, but just stared at the picture of the young soldier that stood upon the sideboard.

"Albert," she whispered, "I know I'll see you again," and with that she put the telegram away and continued to clean the parlour.

Albert had always loved the way she kept everything so spotless, and she'd promised him the day he went away that she would never let her standards fall, and that no matter when he came home, he'd never have reason to complain. A promise she'd kept throughout her life, earning her the title in the village, of 'Molly the Mop', due to the fact that hers was the cleanest kitchen floor anyone had ever seen.

"Thee could eat thee dinner off yer floor," they'd tell her, to which Molly would always reply with a smile, "Well, it would save on the washing up."

She opened her eyes, thinking that she must have left the curtains open before she'd got into bed, as the room was filled with a bright and pinkish light.

"Molly," came a quiet whisper from the side of her bed and, turning to see its origin, she gazed into the eyes of a young man wearing an army uniform.

Molly wasn't the least bit frightened, recognizing his warm smile and shining blue eyes. He knelt down beside her, taking hold of her frail, withered hand and gently kissing the back of it. She acknowledged him.

"Albert," she spoke softly, "I knew you'd come home."

As the implement completed its arc from the back of his head, past the ground - missing the ball entirely…

CHAPTER FIVE

A HUNTING WE WILL GO

Hunting and fishing were part of a countryman's code in Barnsford. Some preferred the rod, some the gun, others the net and ferret, and the more proficient, just about every means available. Like Wilf Jones, for instance, the local poacher, who used what ever it took to put food on the table without having to pay for it.

If Presidents Johnson and Brezhnev had ever decided to put an end to civilization, Wilf would have had the know how - that's providing he could find some buxom country wench who had also survived the holocaust, and didn't find the smell of Wilf too repulsive - to weather the aftermath and repopulate the planet.

Fortunately for Squire Barnsford and the other farmers who enjoyed the benefits of having their own land to take sport from, not everyone was as adept as old Wilf, giving the wildlife that shared their beautiful countryside at least a sporting chance.

Even so, the ineffectiveness of the way some of them carried out their raids upon nature's parlour caused a certain amount of discomfort to some of the poor creatures. It wasn't uncommon to see some angler set on the hope of putting trout upon his breakfast table, chasing a sheep he'd unwittingly hooked while casting his line out around the field; or standing there helpless, as his line flew skywards, caught by some ravenous seagull which had taken the bait in mid-air.

Peter Stewart, local handyman of the parish, decided upon another form of hunting the day he spotted a metal detector in the shop window of a second hand store in Chesham - treasure hunting. Having purchased it for the princely sum of two pounds, three shillings and fourpence, he set off back to Barnsford, certain that within no time at all he would recoup the outlay and be in profit.

The proprietor of the second hand shop always looked forward to Peter's visits. So whenever he walked into his establishment, his face would light up at the prospect of yet another sale that would result in a purchase back at considerably less money than was originally paid within the month.

There had been the record player, that with its huge arm and a needle that was more like a nail held in its great fist, had managed, no matter how many times Peter tried to adjust it, to groove furrows from his collection of Country and Western records. The records had also been bought at the second hand shop, and through the lack of anything to play them on, had never before been heard.

No one at the model aircraft club in Chesham

would ever forget the radio-controlled fighter plane that, thanks to the frequency emitted from the control box, turned a normal club evening into the re-enaction of The Battle Of Britain. It destroyed three Spitfires, two Hurricanes, a Messerschmidt, and a street lamp that lay on the edge of the field at the back of the Chesham British Legion.

Needless to say, Peter's First World War bi-plane survived, and having made a rather clumsy landing on the roof of the club, was able to secure its place back in the second hand shop window at a loss of one pound, five shillings and sixpence.

The golf clubs seemed a good idea at the time. After all, it couldn't be much different from knocking the tops of molehills with his walking stick. This was a feat that Peter had become quite adept at while out on his walks with his dog. So the day he arrived at the Burlington Hall Golf Club, having paid his twenty pounds annual membership subscription, it was with great pride that he took his place on the first tee with Major Bantam, having misinformed the retired army officer, after about ten pints in the Bowlers the previous Saturday night, that he was a dab hand at the old game. The Major had then gone on to inquire what Peter's handicap was, to which he replied, "It was the fact he couldn't walk very far before his knee started to play him up."

The Major still decided, out of the goodness of his heart (and the fact that, being secretary of the club, it was his responsibility to ensure that the membership was increased in order that they could extend the club house), to see that Peter was enrolled as a member before taking him out for a game.

With a bit of coaching from the Major on how to hold his driver, and the general method used for swinging it, Peter, gripped the club as if it were a red-hot poker. He then raised the implement to the heavens, and swung with all his might. As the implement completed its arc from the back of his head, past the ground - missing the ball entirely - and upwards again, it flew out of his limp grasp and headed over the nets put up to stop misguided balls. It continued across the main road, only just missing the top of a passing double-decker bus, and in the direction of the house on the other side of the highway. Here it hit the chimney-stack, bounced back down the roof, dislodging a couple of tiles on its way, and finally came to rest in the guttering to the disgust of the Major who decided to continue playing on his own. Peter had to find his own way from the course, out on to the road and back to the house. Having sheepishly explained to a rather bemused householder as to what he'd done, he offered to pay for the damage caused to the tiles, then borrowed a ladder to retrieve his club.

The following week, the clubs were back in the shop window at a loss of four pounds, ten shillings and fourpence. Although he never played golf again, he did manage, whenever the Major was desperate, to caddy for him in some of the less prestigious competitions the club held. This enabled him to use the premises to drink the beer, which tasted like vinegar, in order to at least give him the satisfaction of knowing he hadn't spent two weeks' hard earned cash for nothing.

The morning after he purchased the metal detector (which turned out to be a beautiful late spring day), Peter packed himself a few sandwiches in some greaseproof paper, and set off in search of undiscovered wealth.

The sun warmed the top of his thinly covered head as he made his way across the fields, following the footpaths as he went. It had occurred to him, as he'd been busy making the preparations for this expedition, that the folk who travelled out to the countryside each weekend, in the hope of finding peace and tranquillity along the same paths that Peter was now treading, had more money than sense! They always ended their walks with a glass or two at the Bowlers, before returning to the opulence of suburbia in their rather expensive-looking motor cars.

They'd appeared to him as the type who treated cash with a great deal less respect than the canny country folk that he had to share the planet with. Not that the man from the second hand shop would agree to that. Nevertheless, it was feasible to our treasure hunter, that when pulling out their maps and guides from their pockets as they picked their way through the countryside (or removed their handkerchiefs to wipe away the sweat from their brows), that money could have poured upon the land like the seed that was sown to grow the crops. With the passing of time, and the cattle that inhabited these fields, this money would have been trodden into the soil, where it was now waiting for Peter to unearth it.

Peter had hardly travelled a hundred yards along the first path when, BZZZZZZZZ, off went the detector. This caused the birds to take to the air, rabbits to bolt down holes, and a small herd of heifers to gallop wildly across the field. They were kicking their back legs in the air as they fled, in the belief they were being chased by a swarm of warble flies.

Getting out the trowel he'd put in his haversack, he dropped to his knees and began digging for all his worth.

After creating a hole about eighteen inches deep and two foot square, he decided that what ever it was, it wasn't money, not unless it had been dropped from an aircraft when the field had been soaking wet. So picking himself up, and kicking the soil back into the hole, Peter carried on, a little bit disappointed, but certainly not discouraged.

Further up the path, moving the machine from side to side and back and forth, the hairs on the back of his neck stood up as yet again the sound pierced the early morning calm: BZZZZZZZ.

Once more he dropped as if hit with a bullet,

trowel in hand before his knees had made contact with the ground.

Once again, the disappointment of five minutes hard toil for nothing.

Two hundred yards further, BZZZZZZ, nothing.

Three hundred yards, BZZZZZZ, nothing.

Four hundred and fifty, BZZZZZZ.

Quarter of a mile; in fact, before he'd even gone a mile, Peter had dug up the equivalent of half a ton of earth, giving the landscape the appearance of having been excavated by a giant mole. All he had to show for it was a brow covered in sweat, and a rather large and painful blister in the centre of his right hand.

"Damn thing must be faulty," he cursed, realising by now that if there had been anything metal in the area he'd just covered, then it certainly hadn't been found by this contraption.

Moving it about in order to see if there was anything obvious about its malfunctioning, he noticed that every time he brought the thing back towards him, it retaliated by piercing his eardrums with its confounded screeching. The nearer it got to his boots, the louder the screech became.

Feeling his face beginning to glow with embarrassment, it suddenly dawned on him as to what the problem might be. Steel toecaps. Yes, he always wore steel toecaps in his boots, and it had been this mass of metal that had been detected by the machine, causing Peter to dig pointlessly for all he was worth.

Not knowing whether to laugh or cry at all the effort he'd put in for nothing, Peter accepted his stupidity in his usual carefree way, and decided to learn from his mistake and carry on; this time making sure that he would hold the detector a good way out in front of him as he made his way along.

After about another half mile or so, the detector started to go wild as Peter scanned it back and forth over a patch of very sandy ground that lay to the side of Barley Wood. Making sure his feet were nowhere near the appliance, he convinced himself that this time he'd found treasure, and once more dropped like a stone and began to dig with all his might.

Finding it a bit futile digging in the sand with his little trowel, with most of the sand pouring back in the hole as fast as he could get it out, Peter threw it to one side, and began scooping out what lay between him and his booty with his bare hands.

After about fifteen minutes, with sweat running down the inside of his clothing as all of last night's alcohol made its way to the surface through the pores in his skin, a three foot deep, and (to stop the sides from collapsing) four foot wide hole now lay gaping up at him. There, lying in the bottom, mockingly, still as shiny as the day it had been manufactured (and probably deposited there by badger baiters who'd wished to conceal the evidence as they made their swift exit from the place), was a garden spade. Although not usually a man to vent his feelings openly, mainly because he was used to life's disappointments, Peter began to turn the air blue with a string of language that would have made even Gus Devenport cringe.

The shovel did come in handy, though, for Peter used it to fill the hole in. Having already got a shovel of his own, it helped to lessen the loss when it was sold to the second-hand shop on the return of the metal detector the following day, this time leaving Peter with a loss of only nineteen shillings and sixpence.

...he'd always considered himself a dab hand when it came to electrics...

CHAPTER SIX

DANGEROUS DAVE

Dangerous Dave was the kind of father every child in the village would have delighted to claim as their own. Though the adults had a different perception on the matter, insisting that he was such a bad influence on his and everyone else's wards, that something ought to be done to bring him to heel.

If nothing else, Bonfire Night last year had been enough to show that his reckless and irresponsible ways were not only a danger to Jack, Mikey, Pete, Alice and Mary - his offspring - but were an imperilment to himself and the whole village.

Having doused the entire bonfire in diesel fuel, Dave continued to pour out a trail of the inflammable liquid all the way up the garden to the back door of the house. This was to enable him to light the pile of old bric-a-brac collected over the last month by the kids, by means of dropping a match on the ground and watching the flame snake its way down the weed-infested back garden to its destination.

Having taken the matches out of his jacket pocket, Dave began to strike them and throw them earthwards in the hope of igniting the trail. Unfortunately, having lost his bearings as he searched for the box of Swan Vestas amongst the bits of string, cigarette packets, sticky sweets and other assorted bits and pieces he kept in there, he'd forgotten whereabouts the trail was. So scattering the matches about the ground in the hope of starting the flame on its way, he had no idea that he was standing, legs akimbo, directly over it.

Whoosh! The flame rose directly upwards from between his legs, licking his testicles like a dog.

"Shit!" came the call of surprise from Dave's lips.

"Yippee!" came the shouts of delight from the kids, as Dave's plan, surprisingly, went according to the way he'd intended it to, the flames leaving his balls alone and racing towards the heap of rubbish, where they caused the bonfire to ignite and leap almost three feet off the ground.

These kids weren't just his own brood but nearly half of the village, who'd come almost expecting a disaster of some form, and knowing that this would be the most exciting celebration of the gunpowder plot in the whole of the county.

The year before had seen the visit of Chesham Fire Brigade who came to put out the fire caused by one of Dave's stray rockets setting fire to Bert Trump's hay stack. Two years ago, Dave had managed to set his own orchard alight. The year before that resulted in a trip to the hospital for this infamous character in order that the hazel nut, having been dropped in the apple bobbing bowl by mistake, could be removed from Dave's nostril, where it had been sucked in during his attempt to show the kids his skill at this age-old custom, combining Halloween with Guy Fawkes night.

Having returned to the celebrations after cooling his backside in a sink full of water, Dave managed to project a rocket through Alec Jones's upstairs window, burning a hole in Mrs Jones's brand new eiderdown, and set fire to Jimmy Stant's new anorak with a lose Catherine Wheel. He caused the clientele at the Bowlers Arms to evacuate the premises when the fumes from the two tractor tyres he'd thrown on the bonfire made their way through an open window, filling the bar with such a putrid aroma that Jack and Doreen had to keep the windows of the pub open for the next two days in order to get rid of the stench.

Dave's disasters weren't just confined to bonfire night. His little altercations with electricity were just as exciting as his exploits with fire.

Jane, his wife, had been on at him for weeks about putting up the fluorescent strip light in the kitchen; so the night she saw flashing blue lights coming from that direction, she just assumed he'd finally got around to doing it.

Dave, however, having discovered earlier that the vacuum cleaner was refusing to pick up the toe nails he'd just clipped, decided to investigate the problem. After all, he'd always considered himself a dab hand when it came to electrics; like the time he'd repaired the broken cable going to the cooker, turning the complete metal casing into a 240 volt conductor, which caused Jane to throw hot chip fat all over the ceiling when she came into contact with the appliance.

Undoing the back of the vacuum, Dave found the reason for this obstinacy on behalf of the cleaner straight away. There, staring at him, was the broken end of the flex.

"Soon 'ave that fixed," he spoke, as though he were addressing a class of electrical students, "just need t' strip the en's agin, and reconnect 'em, an it'll be as good as new."

So, disconnecting the earth and neutral cables of the flex with a good tug, Dave lifted the flex up to his mouth in order to strip the end of the live cable with his teeth. He did most things with his teeth; cut string, pulled off bottle tops, broke the shells off nuts, and all without a single visit to the dentist in thirty-five years. Dave's teeth were as strong and white as elephants' tusks, which he put down to eating plenty of toast and apples.

As he bit deep and hard into the insulation around the flex, he'd failed to notice that the thirteen amp plug was still inserted in the socket. The house lights dimmed, the hair on the top of his head stood on end, and blue flashes were coming from his mouth. This was due to the fact that the cable had firmly wedged between his two front teeth, causing the colour of his face to turn a horrible shade of blue.

At this moment Mikey, Dave's youngest son, walked into the kitchen to get a glass of lemonade. Seeing his father fizzling on the end of a cord, he didn't bother to help, but instead ran upstairs to fetch his brothers and sisters to come and witness for themselves yet another attempt by their father to fascinate them with one of his stunts.

"Quick, come an' see me dad! He's like Herman Munster!"

And as they all stood in the doorway, gazing in disbelief at their father's impression of the Frankenstein's monster character from the kids TV series, Dave finally fell from the stool he'd been sitting on, and pulled the plug from the socket, possibly saving his life in doing so.

So, understandably, it was with great concern that parents would make it clear to their children that they were not allowed to go around and play with the Brookhurst's kids, which could have caused Dave's brood to become social outcasts within the village if any of them had taken any notice of their parents' warnings.

Dangerous Dave, as the kids so fondly nicknamed him, was worshipped by the youngsters, making the Brookhurst children the envy of Barnsford.

Despite his heavy work-load, helping out in his father's tool-making business in Chesham, Dave always found the time to occupy the kids. Making go-carts that would career down the sides of steep hills; building swings in the trees that over-hung the river, and letting them take it in turns to ride his three-fifty James scrambler around the orchard. If their elders ever found out, it would have meant confinement to their home. They made rockets out of gun powder, that on completion they would all take out into the fields beyond Barley Wood; and then, in true NASA tradition, count down before sending them off to their destinations. This usually resulted in the rockets travelling horizontally along the field and into the nearest hedge, very often scattering the ground crew in all directions as they went. This was probably the reason why none of the villagers had ever seen a successful mission, and never knew about the danger their young ones were in. Hidden from view by the trees of Barley Wood, they'd only ever heard the odd explosion, which could have been anything from old farmer Cleggy's gun, to tree roots being blown out on the estate.

Joey Stockton loved heights. If he'd lived on the top floor of The Empire State Building, it would have seemed like paradise. As it was, he had to make do with the attic window of his mother and fathers' house, which over-looked the playing field at the back of the school. So, to make up for it, there was nothing in the surrounding countryside that Joey wouldn't attempt to scale: trees, haystacks, flagpoles, telegraph poles, on to the roofs of sheds, old deserted buildings; in fact, anywhere that could prove a challenge to this seven-year-old mountaineer. So the day that Joey slipped out of the back door of the school, after going to the toilet to relieve himself from his aching bladder and the boredom of lessons, the sight of the sun gleaming against the cockerel-featured weather vane on the top of the church tower issued to the lad a dare he couldn't resist.

Opening the big church door and finding the place deserted, Joey made his way up the steep stone steps that led to the bell tower. Entering the sanctity of this place of such pleasure to the villagers, Joey closed the door behind him and slid the large rusty bolt across, in order that no one should interrupt him on his quest.

Then, squeezing through the small open slit that let light into the place, he clambered out and onto the sandstone parapet that ran around the outer edge of the tower. From here Joey could just reach the top wall of the tower itself, and gripping the stone with his tiny fingers, he managed to haul himself up and on to the pinnacle of the house of God.

Joey felt pleased with himself, and remained up there for a good half hour, peeping through the gaps of the turret at the folk going about their business below.

He'd have probably have stayed there for the whole of the morning if hunger hadn't taken hold of him. So, deciding to go down and surrender himself to Mr Bennion the headmaster, Joey clambered over the wall and tried to lower himself back down onto the parapet.

Joey couldn't understand what had happened; maybe he'd shrunk with hunger, perhaps he'd broken the ledge as he'd pushed himself up to climb over in the first place. Whatever the reason, the parapet appeared to have gone, and his little legs were now kicking and lashing about in mid-air in the hope of finding something to lower himself down on to.

Mustering up every ounce of strength from within his small undeveloped body, Joey managed to pull himself back up and over the battlements; from whence, having given himself time to regain his breath, his cries for help echoed across the entire countryside.

Mrs Morris, his form teacher, had only just finished her enquiries of the two boys she'd sent to find Joey, when through the open window of the classroom came the pathetic cries of her pupil. Looking out of the window in the direction of the whining call, she could just make out the head of a child peeping through the battlement on the summit of Barnsford church.

Not being sure whether they were the beatific looks of an Angel, or the twisted tormented features of a Gargoyle, she went out into the playground to investigate further.

By the time Mrs Morris had reached the church gates, a small crowd had already gathered in the street, including Joey's mother, who was making her way back from Tom Stanworth's, the butcher's shop, when she'd heard the cries for assistance from her son.

"Hang on lad," came a reassuring voice from out of the crowd. "We'll get thee down," and with that, Percy Briggs, who just happened to be enjoying a day off from his employment as post master in Chesham, ran into the church and up the stairs to the bell tower.

Finding the door into the tower locked, Percy tried with all his might to force it open. But for all the good it seemed to do, he might as well have been trying to move a mountain.

It was a frantic mother who saw Percy reappear in the doorway of the church, having to admit that his rescue attempt had met with defeat, but reassuring Mrs Stockton that it would only take a phone call and within half an hour Chesham Fire Brigade would be on the scene.

It was at that moment that Dangerous Dave put in an appearance, with his neck in a collar due to the accident he'd had at his father's works; which was lucky for Dave because, only a week before, he'd taken out a personal insurance policy against such cases.

"What's the matter?" he enquired.

"Little Joey Stockton's climbed up on to the tower, an' the door t' the bell tower's locked, an the lad conner git down," one of the ladies standing in the crowd explained, breathless from trying to relate the story before anyone else could.

"Percy's goin' t' ring fer Fire Brigade, but it wunner be here fer another half-hour," another informed him, feeling quite pleased there'd been some of the story left to tell.

Dave had always had a soft spot for young Joey, seeing in him the adventurer that lay within his own character. But ever since the time the lad had returned from a visit to Dave's house with ripped trousers (caused by falling out of Dave's apple tree), Joey had been banned from ever visiting Dave's place again. In fact, Mrs Stockton had been round to Doug Billbrook's, the local bobby's place, and warned him that if nothing was done about his irresponsibility, he'd have the serious injury of some child on his conscience. Doug gave Dave a warning, which only had the effect of hurting the man's feelings, but other than that, danger continued to be attached to everything that Dave did.

Maybe it was time to put that cavalier approach to life to the ultimate test, win over the hearts of all his critics and become the hero he'd always dreamt of being, he thought to himself, as everyone else stood round looking helpless.

Back home in the shed at the back of his house lay his latest attempt at space travel. Made up from cardboard tubes, a garden cane, gun powder, tissue paper, and all held together with string and tape, it stood awaiting a test flight. But what better way to prove his ability as a rocketeer, than to use his skills to rescue young Joey Stockton, and in front of the whole village?

"Don't worry, I'll get 'im down. I just need sumit from wome fost," and with that he turned and set off in the direction of his house as if it was on fire.

"What the bloody hell's he goin' t' do now?" a petrified Joey's mother enquired of one her neighbours. "As if he anner caused enough trouble encouraging the kids t' do these daft things in fost place!" and, starting to cry at the thought of her young lad marooned on top of the church, Mrs Stockton had to be comforted by her friends as they awaited the return of Dangerous Dave.

In no time at all Dave was back, carrying with him the missile that, with a bit of luck (and Dave was sure he was due a bit), would soon make him the saviour of little Joey Stockton, and a celebrity throughout the whole village.

"What the bloody hell 'ave yer gotten there?" Harry Gittins enquired.

"Its an 'ome-made rocket, an if thee gives us an 'and, I'm goin' t' aim it over the church with this 'ere piece of fishing line attached to it. Then, we'll tie this 'ere rope t' line, an' pull it over the tower an' I'll climb up an' get thee lad down," he explained calmly, as if it was an everyday operation.

The crowd looked at Dave as if he were mad, but with no better idea of their own, had to agree it was worth a go.

Propping the rocket against an old wooden box

that he'd made Arthur Blake, the grocer, go and fetch, Dave aimed it in the direction of the church, and testing the force and direction of the wind with a wet finger, was revelling in the theatrical.

"If me calculations is rit, then it should just clear the tower and land in Mrs Merton's garden, enabling me t' tie it to a tree in 'er orchard and then scale the tower from this side."

Clearing everyone back to a safe distance, Dave took out a box of matches from the back pocket of his trousers. Having found a good one from the many dead ones that had been put back in the box, he struck it and lit the touch paper.

The flame shot up the tissue paper like lightening, barely giving him time to get clear himself, and with an almighty *whoosh*, it left the ground - setting alight the box as it did.

Swerving its way upward, to everyone's surprise, the rocket headed in the general direction of the church. Clipping the head of the cockerel on the weather vane as it passed, it spun the metal bird round so severely that it flew from its perch as though given life and crashed to the ground below, where it bounced off one of the old medieval tombstones and ricocheted through the stained glass window, taking the head clean off a Crusader, something the Saracen he'd been fighting had been unable to do for the last seven hundred years or so.

As it dipped and headed earthwards on the other side, the crowd cheered as if they'd just witnessed the first successful British Space Flight. Dave's face glowed with pride.

"Rit, tie the rope t' end of line, an' I'll go round t'other side and pull it over and tie it up," Dave gave the instructions, taking command now of the entire situation and finding he was getting the respect of all who'd gathered there to watch.

Disappearing round the back of the church, everyone watched as the rope snaked its way towards heaven as if it were a snake charmer's cobra, and then after a spell of about five minutes, Dave returned to the throng to play his part in the heroic rescue.

After a bit of an argument with Percy Briggs as to who was going to climb up, Dave, allowing no one to spoil his big moment, removed his neck brace, grabbed the rope, and began his ascent of the church.

Having made it to the top after a breathtaking couple of minutes, to the cheers of the villagers, he very gently lowered young Joey down through the small opening and back into the bell tower. Then, having forced his own frame through the narrow opening, unbolted the door and led the lad down the stairs and out of the front door into the waiting arms of his mother – that's, of course, after she'd clipped the little lad around the ear hole first.

Dave received the adulation of the crowd with all the humility of a film star, and was about to give leave to his fans, when Mrs Merton (having been one of the first to leave the scene of Dave's triumph), returned to the front door of her cottage and, with her best scolding voice, bellowed across the green at our celebrity.

"Dave Brookhurst, just you come an' look at what yer bloody rocket's done t' me greenhouse!"

Danny woke the following morning to the sound of a cockerel crowing on Mr Randles' farm next door...

CHAPTER SEVEN

HEARTS OF OAK

"Are you my Daddy?" Danny inquired, gazing into the eyes of the man standing at his Grandad Elliot's garden gate.

With a drooping bushy moustache, and a face so weary and weather beaten, it could almost have been hewn from the old oak that stood in the field at the back of his Grandfather's house, the stranger had the appearance of a man far more advanced in years than he actually was.

Draped in a worn-out khaki overcoat, and with a rather heavy-looking haversack thrown over his slightly rounded shoulders, he peered down at the boy. Who, though he'd never had the joy of cuddling him, he could tell from the reflection he'd so often seen in his shaving mirror, was the child that had been blessed to him and his wife while he'd been away serving the King on the battlefields of France.

Although not a big man, he appeared to this small four-year-old as if he were a giant. But despite the rough exterior of three days' growth on his unshaven face, there was a warmth and gentleness about his appearance that gave Danny a feeling of assurance as he stood there, smiling at him, while the lad hopped nervously from one foot to the other.

The Great War had deprived Danny of his father's presence during his infancy. But likewise it had also robbed this tired and battle-worn man of the chance to watch his first male offspring grow, into what could only be described, now, as a chubby, cheeky, likeness of his own self. He was also absent when needed to help his grieving wife bury their nameless other son, Danny's twin brother, who'd died only a few days after his birth.

He'd never been put on this earth to be a soldier, for God had blessed him with the ability to build structures out of bricks. If he wasn't doing that, he tended the land on his own father's farm at Burley Bank which, according to the Squire (Grandad Jones's landlord), had been rented out to their family for as far back as records cared to show. Nevertheless, a soldier he'd been for the last four years, and it had been this War to end all Wars that had taken him away from his family.

Now, on a cold and frosty morning in the January of 1920, after seeing so much of death and destruction, he had returned. Knowing, like so many men of his generation, that life to him in this small farming community would never be the same again.

Unemployed, and not having the money to set up home for themselves, Danny's mother and father had begun their married lives living with her father and younger sister, Cissie, at Manor View, where, along with his elder sister Doreen, Danny had come to consider this house his home.

Granny Elliot was still alive, but due to what was put down to the change of life, she had been admitted to a home for the mentally disturbed in Chesham.

She had developed a form of religious mania, and although, like most folk of that period, Danny's Grandad liked to think of himself as a God-fearing Christian, it hadn't stopped him from having her interned for trying to give away the family savings to the church.

Taking early retirement from his job as Post Master at Chesham, Mr Elliot had moved with his family to Barnsford, where, when his two sons married and left home, Cissie, the eldest of the girls became the bread-winner, working as the cook at the Hall.

Danny's father had suffered from gas poisoning, shrapnel wounds, and a complete mental breakdown from the horrors he'd witnessed. Now, with his health improving, and reunited with his family, he knew it was time to try and put all that behind him, procure a job, find a home of their own, and get on with the task of rebuilding his life and raising the next generation of Joneses.

The rain beat against the window panes and the wind whistled under the door, causing the flames of the fire to dance upon the coals that were sustaining their life. Danny's father stood there, trying as best he could to hold back the bout of coughing that was beginning to take hold of his body. With water running down his mackintosh, causing a moat to form on the bare stone floor around him, he waited in the office at Barnsford Hall estate yard, with his cap in his hand as the Estate Manager made up his mind as to whether the Squire's budget could afford yet another burden to its already large payroll.

Despite having faced the might of the German army, believing his chances of ever seeing his family again were remote, his fears had been nothing to the churning feeling his stomach was experiencing as the futures of not only himself, but his wife, Danny, and Danny's elder sister, Doreen, were now being decided.

It would have only taken one of the thousands upon thousands of bullets and shells that were flying through the air, like gnats on a summer's evening, to snuff out his short life. But at least he knew he was being paid, and therefore able to support his wife and children back home. But now, demobbed, unemployed, and having spent the last twelve months convalescing from the mental torture of war, what use would he be to anyone if he failed to find work? He might as well have been killed back there on the battlefields of France, he thought, trying to hide the expectancy that was causing his body to tremble like a leaf in a cold

November wind.

He could feel the beads of sweat, intermingling with the water that had fallen upon him from the heavens, running down his rounded but powerful back. The Estate Manager browsed over the work sheets, caring little for the fact that this man had risked his life fighting for the King (whose very portrait was hanging over the same fire that had kept him warm all the while Danny's father had been up to his knees in the filth of human waste within the trenches).

"You say you're a bricklayer by trade?"

"Aye, Sir, but I know about farming, and I'm prepared t' put me 'and t' owt."

The Estate Manager surveyed Danny's father from head to toe, as though he were enjoying the anxiety he was causing this proud man, and then turning back to his paper work, without even bothering to look at him as he spoke, he gave the man the news he'd been praying for.

"Start Monday. I'll put yer to building some artificial fox lairs in the woods. If yer do a good job, I might think of takin' yer on permanent."

Danny's father never felt the rain as he walked home, he was too happy to care. But Danny still remembers his sore and chapped face as he burst through the door, and, grabbing his wife, swung her round and kissed her.

"Joseph, behave thee sen, not while the kids are watchin'."

"But Lydia, I've gotten a job, and on Monday

when I starts, I'm going t' see if there's any chance of gettin' that cottage on the estate that me dad told me about."

So, with a job found, the rent of the cottage agreed upon, Danny's father prepared his family for the move to their first family home.

"Whoa, boy!" Danny yelled at the horse, a hint of self-importance in his squeaky voice, having been entrusted with the responsibility of holding firm Grandad Jones' old grey mare, 'Poppy', while his parents loaded their belongings onto the cart. He was exercising his authority by showing her who was boss, and although the horse wouldn't have moved an inch without being forced to, it didn't stop Danny from emulating the orders he'd so often heard the men in the fields give to their charges.

"Hold fast, there!" he called. "Back, back!" he continued, as the old girl just looked down at him with a twinkle in her eye, and what could have easily have been mistaken for a smile upon her large rubbery lips.

The warm sunshine licked the back of Danny's neck like the kitten Aunty Cissie had given him, filling him with excitement at the prospect of the great adventure that lay ahead. As he stared at his muscular father, struggling with a few bits and pieces of furniture onto the back of the old wooden cart that had been donated by Aunty Cissie, Grandad Elliot, and one or two well-wishing neighbours, Danny felt safe in the knowledge that here was a man who'd fought the entire German army, and won.

He'd been to see the house with his mother; in fact, he'd spent most of the previous week helping to scrub the floors, wash down the paint work, and blacken the fire grates that occupied every room. Not that they were all that dirty to begin with, as the last occupiers had gone through exactly the same procedure the day they had vacated the place. But like all women of that era, unable to afford the luxury of re-decorating, it was her way of laying down her scent, like a cat who had to scratch its mark upon some tree it wished to claim. Danny, although knowing what to expect, still felt excited at the prospect of his own room, and the thought of his father joining the landed gentry (which gave our little would-be farmer such a buzz, that it was right now causing butterflies to wheel and spin around his stomach).

High up in an old crab apple tree, a goldfinch burst into song, as it too began the arduous chore of setting up home. As Danny and his family made their way proudly towards their new lodgings, they noticed that all along the hedgerows of the narrow twisting lanes, other small creatures of the wing were also preparing their shelters in expectation of their forth-coming families.

Danny's father lifted the rickety old gate of Grafton Cottage up on its hinges and, dragging it open, commented to his wife that its repair would be one of the first jobs on his list.

Danny looked down the path towards the front door, and as the reflection of the sun glinted off one of the upstairs windows, it was as if the house was winking at him, beckoning him to come on in. If God had built them all a castle, high above a green and fertile valley, with as much land as the eye could see, it couldn't have made them feel any more blessed than they all felt that morning.

Danny's mother gazed into the eyes of her husband, peered down at their two healthy young offspring and burst out crying.

"Joe," she addressed young Danny's father, "I feel as if I've fallen asleep and woke up in Paradise."

"Aye, Lydia, I knows what tha means. It's what yo' an' me always talked about when we was courtin'. And now its 'appened, but it duner 'arf make me wonder what else tha Lord's gotten in store fer us all."

With that, they made their way up the path, where, reaching the front door, Danny's father whisked his wife off her feet, and with the children giggling at the sight of their mother in Father's arms like that, carried her over the threshold.

Danny woke the following morning to the sound of a cockerel crowing on Mr Randles' farm next door, and as he rubbed the sleep away from his half-opened eyes, he peered about his new bedroom, bewildered at finding himself there..

Suddenly remembering the move, he leapt out of bed and raced to the window to peer out at the countryside that lay at the back of the cottage, a vista that would have made Angels sing.

His dad was downstairs having a quick swill in the old cracked Belfast sink in the kitchen. As Danny peered around the door at his father, he noticed how red and brown his arms, neck and face were compared to the rest of his torso, which was as white as the snow. Not really understanding what the great red marks that lay upon the pale flesh of his father's back and sides were, Danny thought how clever his mother had been to have bought a vest that covered his father's white bits so well. No wonder he rarely took it off; in fact, he thought, Dad looked a bit like one of Mr Cooper's Ayrshire cows.

Breakfast devoured, Danny rushed outside to begin the exploration of this new world. First he wandered into the orchard already full of blossom, which, providing the finches left well alone, would mean plenty of belly-ache for Danny in future months.

Next he wandered into the outbuildings, where the coal and sticks for the fire were piled high, as if in anticipation of a bad winter.

Having done his reconnaissance of the place quicker than he'd scheduled, Danny forgot all about his mother's instructions to stay within calling distance, and decided that Mr Randles' farm next door was also in need of surveying. So, crawling under the rusty barbed-wire fence that separated the two properties, he made his way through the discarded implements that had been left at the back of the farm until they were next needed. He made his way around the manure heap (had he fallen in, it would probably have eaten him whole), past the hen shed, through the stack yard (which at that precise moment contained the biggest Hereford bull Mr Randles had ever owned), and out into the paddock at the far side of the farm. Here lay the remnants of a large fire that had been used to destroy the residue from the hedge-cutting around the paddock.

Danny wandered over, kicking up the dust from the now day-old cinders that had scorched the earth. Sticking out his leg to boot an old charred can, he hooked it on a brier that had crept its way along the grass from the hedgerow at the side. Then just as his leg reached its maximum, the brier snatched at his ankle, causing the little lad to topple into the ash.

Danny fell headlong into the ash, covering his arms with the burning powder, and causing the pain to stretch the skin to the point of splitting.

The screams of the youngster echoed across the farm and back to the cottage. In less than five minutes, Danny's mother raced to the rescue of her injured son, and had him back home with his arms fully immersed in a vat of buttermilk.

Bandaging up the poor lad's limbs, Doctor Price told Lydia how her quick reactions had saved Danny from being scarred for life. But, as Doctor Price closed the door behind him, Lydia looked at her son, who by now had seemed to have forgotten his injuries and was teasing the cat on the rug. As she gazed at this extension of her own self, she couldn't help but worry about the fearlessness that, just like her husband, Danny appeared to possess, and she wondered what other dangers life held in store for her four-year-old boy.

Dan leaned his crutch against the bar, and with his strong arms, lifted himself up on to the bar-stool.

"A pint of yer best, John," he ordered, and with lips that never uttered a single moan, formed a smile that would have melted ice.

"How's tha leg t'day?" John Wilson enquired, whereat Dan (who although suffering a great deal of pain, never talked much about his missing limb, lost while rescuing a fellow soldier in the Second World War), just laughed and replied, "I dunner know, I anner seen it fer twenty odd years!"

"Right, who's had the Land Rover?" Dennis demanded. In turn, each of the crew, winking at each other...

CHAPTER EIGHT

DENNIS GOUGH

It had taken Dennis Gough a great deal longer to settle in as the new manager on Barnsford Estate than he'd expected, finding Barry Whiteford, his predecessor, a rather hard act to follow. The hardest part was trying to make himself understood by the workforce; a workforce that varied so much personality-wise, that it made him wonder whether he'd inherited the post of commander-in-chief of some multinational task force.

It ranged from the eloquent vocabulary of Tarquin Jones, known by the rest of his work chums as the 'Welsh wizard of the vernacular', whose curriculum vitae read like an over-worked schizophrenic. Publican, circus entertainer, professional footballer, soldier, actor, rock and roll singer, and now, after moving to Barnsford with his family, labourer on the Squire's estate. Here, despite his many stories on just about every aspect possible (told with such a sweet and educated Welsh dialect to Arthur Dawlish and Doug Jones, at sixty five and sixty three respectively, two of the oldest men on the payroll), it was impossible to prove that anything he related to the men was false.

When Dennis had first encountered Arthur and Doug, they were laying a concrete stockyard on one of the Squire's farms. Standing to listen to their conversation on the progress of the job, he found that the content of the confabulation contained about as much word-stock as the meeting of two aliens from differing parts of the Galaxy.

"Tha's not street, tha knows," began Doug, referring to the level of the tampered cement.

"I bet thee in," replied Arthur sharply, never happy when anyone criticized his ability,

"I bet thee inner," argued Doug, stubbornly.

"I bet thee in." Once again Arthur corrected him.

"I bet thee inner," Doug insisted once more, determined that he was going to have the last word.

"I bet thee in," continued Arthur, getting more and more annoyed at this consistent nit-picking.

"I bet thee inner," Doug hit back before Arthur had time to draw in fresh breath, and, thinking he'd won the day, was swatted by a rather breathless, "In," from Arthur that took the wind right out of Doug's sails.

"Well, I bet I con git it streeter," insisted Doug, having paused momentarily for breath.

"I bet thee conner," Arthur replied very

indignantly at this second challenge to his ability to eye a job up.

"I bet I con."

"I bet thee conner."

"I bet I con."

"I bet thee conner."

"I bet I con."

"I bet thee conner."

"Well, I bet if I put another couple of barrer loads down that end, it'll git it level," continued Doug, not going to be fobbed off by this old bugger.

"Well, I bet it dunner," once again Arthur disputed, not letting this young upstart get the last word.

"I bet it dun."

"I bet it dunner."

"I bet it dun."

"I bet it dunner."

"I bet it dun."

"I bet it dunner."

"I bet old mon Barnsford notices it," carried on Doug, hoping to appeal to Arthur's pride.

"I bet he wunner," came Arthur's reply, still convinced that there was nothing to notice.

"I bet he wun."

"I bet he wunner."

"I bet he wun."

"I bet he wunner."

"I bet he wun."

"I bet he wunner."

Just as it looked to Dennis that this argument was going to last until one of the two old timers dropped dead, young Martin Speers, the plumber's apprentice, called out to the bickering labourers that the kettle had just boiled. Tea was about to be served up within the confines of the pig pen, which had been transformed, by a few rickety chairs they'd found about the old farmhouse, a plank of wood supported by two oil drums which acted as a table, forming a scullery the men would have been proud enough to have allowed their womenfolk to use.

With that news, Doug turned to Arthur, realising that by the end of tea break the concrete would be well on the way to going off, and succumbing to the elder labour's experience, held out his arms in surrender and said, "Well, I suppose a blind mon on a galloping hos wouldner notice it."

Arthur, showing very little jubilation over what had been a hard-earned victory, shrugged his shoulders and replied, "Now, I doubt he would," and with that they both downed their tools and made their way across to the old barn for 'snappin', laughing and wheezing like a pair of old bellows.

One thing that irritated Dennis about the men on Barnsford Estate was the way, after spending hours going over what he wanted on a job, pointing out in every little detail the 'ins' and 'outs' of this and that, they would just look at him, smile, and then say, as if humouring him, "I thinks I knows what tha means, Mr Gough." Then they carried on doing the job the way that they saw fit, not giving a hoot about time, the amount of materials used, or how many of them it took to carry the task out.

The result was always the same, with the Squire complimenting the men at the end on a job well done, and Dennis, despite having informed the Squire that it could have been done faster and cheaper, if they'd done this, or that, admitting that it did look a fine piece of artistry when all was said and done.

The Squire himself was just as frustrating as the men, always giving Dennis the most extraordinary requests. Just like the time he told him where to put the light fitting in the kitchen of a farmhouse they were refurbishing. Dennis, noticing that it was well off-centre of the room, questioned the Squire as to whether he was certain that that was where he wanted it to go, and was given the kind of reply that he would soon become used too.

"S-s-see that b-b-barn over there?"

Dennis peered out of the kitchen window, and gazed across the farmyard at the barn that lay to the far side.

"Yes," he said, somewhat bewildered as to what a building that lay over fifty yards away had to do with the position of the kitchen light.

"W-w-well," continued the Squire, whose stammer always meant the men having to wait in anticipation for whatever gem he would come out with next, "It l-lines up p-p-perf-fectly with t-that." And with that he turned round and made his way into the next room. Here he continued to inform Dennis as to where every stick of furniture would be placed, and, without any consultation with the occupants, gave the orders to his second-in-command as to where every plug socket and light switch would go.

Then there was the time Dennis had arrived at a job to find Bill Dutton, the plumber who, on the Squire's instructions, had run the pipes a foot off the ceiling, across the centre of the kitchen, and upon pointing out to the old man that in his opinion it didn't look right, was told:

"It w-w-will be al-r-right for hanging their s-socks on, to dry."

Dennis, who'd spent over five years training in the art of the building trade, studying the building regulations, architecture, surveying and design, could only stand there flabbergasted as the old man destroyed everything he'd been taught and believed in.

The day Dennis took possession of his brand new Land Rover was a proud day for him. Although it was to be used by the workforce in general, he never missed a chance to be out in it, riding through the leafy lanes, or along Barnsford High Street as though he were the Squire himself. Despite the vehicle being for common purpose, Dennis became obsessed with it, and treated the machine as if it were his own little toy.

Jumping into it one hot summer's day, as it lay parked outside the office, he drove around the corner of the yard buildings. Setting off to visit one of the farms, he was stopped in his tracks by Mrs Turner, the Squire's trusted secretary.

"Mr Gough, the Squire wants to see you right away. I rang the office, but you'd just left."

"What's he want now?" Dennis enquired, rather flustered because of the workload he'd set himself for the day.

"I don't know, he didn't say, but it sounded urgent," Mrs Turner replied hesitantly.

Dennis parked the Land Rover tightly up against the side of the Hall, and, with the engine still running, left the vehicle in the full blaze of the sun while he entered the Squire's private office to receive his instructions. Probably to tell him he'd changed his mind again over something or other.

"Ah, Gough, s-s-sit down. I w-w-want to discuss the new b-barn at Barley Farm."

After nearly an hour of listening to the Squire, rambling on about how he was going to erect this new concrete and metal construction whether the council gave their permission or not, Dennis was given leave of the old man and left with his head spinning. So much so, that he'd completely forgotten where or what he'd been doing, but also forgetting about the Land Rover, which was still purring away alongside the Hall wall, the sun beating down on the canvas top and the windows acting like a heat exchanger. He wandered back to his own office in the hope of picking up the pieces of what had now become another unorganised day.

Back in his office, he gathered together his wits, and deciding to move onto something different, went outside his office to where he expected the Land Rover to be standing.

"Who's had the damn Land Rover?" he demanded of Bob Black, as the joiner was making his way across the yard to the tool shed.

"I dunner know, Mr Gough," Bob replied, knowing full well, like the rest of the men who were down at the yard, that it was outside the Hall with the motor still running.

"Well get the men in my office. I want to get the matter of who has taken the Land Rover, and when, straight with them!" he ordered, and with that, he turned on his heels and went back into the office, huffing and puffing to himself.

Within ten minutes, Dennis's office was heaving with the workforce of Barnsford Estate, who, through lack of big jobs to be on, were back at the yard tidying up the ends of one or two tasks.

"Right, who's had the Land Rover?" Dennis demanded. In turn, each of the crew, winking at each other, denied knowing anything about its whereabouts.

"Well, if nobody knows where they've left it, we'd better get out there and search for it."

So leading them out of the office, with a threat that, if they weren't more responsible for the

Estate equipment, then they would have to be made accountable for everything that they took out from now on. They all followed him around the corner like sheep, until coming into the courtyard at the back of the Hall; there, parked up and well disguised against the ivy that was growing up the wall, was the green Land Rover, engine still running.

What Dennis didn't know, and he was the only one that didn't, was that Stan Wilson, one of the bricklayers, had seen it parked there while Dennis was with the Squire, and opening the door, had reached in and turned the heater on and up to full as a bit of a practical joke, thinking that when Dennis came out of the Squire's office, the cab would be so hot, it would bowl him over upon opening the door.

Almost an hour and a half later the engine was still ticking away, and Dennis, who raced ahead of the others in the hope that he could turn it off before anyone noticed found to his discomfort, as the blistering heat hit him full in the face, that it was like the inside of a furnace.

The men, not letting Dennis get too far ahead, had all broken into a trot behind him, so within seconds of their gaffer's arrival at the vehicle, they were all gathered around him.

"Bloody hell, Mr Gough, it's bloody wharm in 'ere," Bill Dutton, the plumber, commented.

"Aye", agreed Bob Black, "tha could grow tomatoes in this heat."

Dennis, who'd managed to turn off the engine before the men had caught up with him, explained that it must be the heat of the sun, shining through the windows, that had caused the clammy atmosphere which had enveloped the cab. With the men agreeing with him in their usual servile, but nevertheless sarcastic, way, they turned on their heels and headed for an early brew, knowing damn' well that nothing would be said in the way of a reprimand. In fact, for the rest of the week at least, early and long breaks would be taken without so much as a care as to what Mr Gough might say; that was if he didn't want reminding about the need to be careful where the Estate equipment was left, and the necessity of conserving fuel in the name of economising.

...he'd invite them into the dark interior of the forge then, seating them on a plank spread between two used oil drums... would proceed to tell them stories.

CHAPTER NINE

THE BLACKSMITH

"The Blacksmith was a mighty man,
his balls were made of iron,
and jangled as he ran."

Tom Barton had been the subject of this verse the kids were now singing outside his smithy since the day he'd taken over the business on his father's retirement - over thirty five years ago.

Although he'd heard this song (then aimed at his dad), ever since he was a small child, he'd never got tired of the glee in successive generations of children's faces, as at first he watched his old man, and now he himself was given the duty of pursuing them up the street in the pretence that he was annoyed.

The smithy was a place of magic for the children, with flames roaring into the air as the bellows were pumped to get the coals as hot as they'd go. Sparks spitting upwards off the hot metal, where they'd briefly light up the horseshoe-laden beams, before dying out and dropping back down to earth as merely cold pieces of burnt-out filings. The smell of scorched metal and bone as a horse was shod, the crackling of the fuel in the forge and, as though he were a sorcerer mixing his potions, the sight of the Blacksmith himself as differing forms of light flickered across his sweaty, grimy face, playing tricks with the young minds of all who stood watching in the doorway. They were fascinated as the mighty arms of the smith rose and fell to the beat of the hammer, first with a little click upon the anvil, and then, lifting the tool of his trade higher, with a powerful smack upon the metal he was working into shape.

Tom was in fact a mighty man; as for his balls, well, despite the kiddies' rhyme, they were flesh and blood the same as his father's. Although maybe the sound of the nails in the front of his leather apron as he playfully chased them up the street could have been the cause of this mistaken belief.

If he wasn't being plagued by their song, or his daily schedule wasn't too demanding, he'd invite them into the dark interior of the forge then, seating them on a plank spread between two used oil drums (a kind of home-made theatre), would proceed to tell them stories. Tales that had been told to him by his father about knights and kings, about magic, and how Barnsford had once been the site of King Arthur's Camelot, where his ancestors had shod the horses of the brave men of the Round Table before they rode out to do battle with some evil sorcerer, or to slay a dragon that had been terrorising the neighbouring villages.

There he would sit amid the dancing light; and, totally forgetting about his workload, would amuse the kids until it was time to close up. Then, rising to his feet with a roar that would put fear into larger hearts than these, he would shout, "I wish yo lot'd bugger off. I've gotten work t' do, an yer dads 'l not thank me if their tools anner fixed."

At which the children would scamper to their feet and, pouring out of the smithy doorway into the street, would once again burst into rhyme in the hope that Tom would chase them up the road.

Thinking of Tom's stories as they excitedly made their way home for tea, they felt as though they'd almost been there, watching, as the knights came and went from the smithy, riding out towards whatever quest the King had set them.

"Farewell, Smith!" cried one, as he hauled the great weight of the chain mail and armour he was encased in, up and onto his steed. "Just off to rescue a damsel in distress, but if I should survive, I'll buy yer a pint in The Bowlers later."

"Well, mind as you go," replied Tom's ancestor, as the gallant Sire rode off; and, passing the 'Get It All' grocery shop, rounded the bend by the Bowlers, then disappeared along the tarmac road towards Chesham.

Billy Thomas once swore blind after one of these story-telling sessions, that he'd actually seen King Arthur and his men ride from out of Bickerty Hill, just as Tom had told them he would if ever

England needed them, and seeing as the National football team were to meet Germany in the World Cup Final that following Saturday, he reckoned this had been the reason for their sudden appearance. But later, agreeing with his playmates, who were jealous that it wasn't them who had witnessed the scene, admitted that it could have been old man Cleggie's cattle, being frightened back into the field by a fox; and he didn't mention the subject again for fear of being further ridiculed or beaten.

The kids hung on every word Tom spoke, and so, between Dangerous Dave and the Smith, throughout the school holidays, their parents only ever saw them at meal and bed times.

Tony Clark was almost fifteen, and with the thought of leaving school ever-present in his mind, told Tom one day that he'd like to be a blacksmith like him.

"Tha dunner wanner be that," Tom advised him. "Tha'll always be toiling and never git t' see the light of day."

But Tony's mind was made up, and he told Tom he was going to apply for a job in the foundry at Chesham where his uncle worked.

"Well," said Tom one day, after trying again to put the lad off, "tha' better see if tha's up t it," and with that, he handed the lad the hammer. Putting a piece of flat metal in the coals, he told him that when it was hot enough, then he could strike the object on his command, then together they could work it into shape.

"Rit," said Tom. "When I say, strike, yo 'it it as 'ard as thee con."

"OK," Tony agreed, and with that, Tom shouted out the command.

"Strike!"

The hammer came down upon the metal with all the might young Tony could muster

"Strike!"

Yet again the lad struck the object, only this time he felt the blow shudder all the way up his arm.

Composing himself just in time, the order rang through the smithy again.

"Strike!"

And once again the lad stuck for all his worth.

They must have been at it for fifteen minutes, Tom yelling out his commands, and Tony, sweat pouring down both his face and back from every pore in his body, making his thin white tee shirt stick to his back, answering each call with a strike that would have made Tom's dad proud; even if for the last five minutes or so, each strike was becoming weaker and weaker.

The lad looked at the Blacksmith and asked, "What are we making, Mr Barton?"

"What does it look like, lad?" Tom enquired, smiling at the expression of fatigue etched on the lad's face.

"A frying pan," Tony answered, not really sure, but by the way he was looking at it through hazed-over eyes, it did look remotely like one.

"OK," Tom said, rubbing his chin questioningly and, looking down into the lad's tired face, he smiled, and giving him a mischievous wink and a pat on the head, patronizingly continued, "We'll make a frying pan."

Climbing on board the punt, the gang transformed into a crew of pirates, setting out to terrorise these treasure-laden waters.

CHAPTER TEN

THE HOLE IN THE HEDGE GANG

"Six of the best."

That was the gang motto, and by placing their fists one on top of the other, they'd echo this whenever they meant business.

The James Boys, The Hole In The Wall Gang, Ma Baker and her boys, Bonnie and Clyde, had all in their turn taken it upon themselves to spread terror and mayhem throughout the territory. But none had ever struck fear into the hearts of the people like The Hole In The Hedge Gang, known for the way they always entered their victims' property, usually by a hole made in the hedge.

The gang leader was a ruthless varmint by the name of Billy Jones and, although only ten years of age, he was as cunning and daring as any outlaw who ever crossed over to the other side of the law.

Following the unfortunate death at the hands of a rusty hay turner of last year's school delinquent, Andy Lea, Billy had seized upon the chance of replacing this infamous character on moving up to his final year at Barnsford Primary. Although

Andy had been as cunning as any scoundrel could be, he had been a loner. But despite this, he had remained Billy's, and all the school's, hero.

Billy however, had the support of his gang, giving him more scope for exercising greater havoc upon the law-abiding citizens of Barnsford, as well as someone to share the blame.

Billy was a good-looking lad, with his bright red bedraggled hair, and his freckly face giving anyone who met him the impression that butter wouldn't melt in his mouth. And yet, despite the twinkle in his soft brown eyes, behind them his mind was working overtime on what could be his next prank.

As for the rest of the gang, they had been selected for their loyalty towards Billy, and the fact that, due to not being able to think for themselves, they would play their part in any plan Billy had in mind.

There was Scar Face Bailey, known for the mark left under his right eye from the day he tripped over his mother's cat and cut it open on the edge of the coal scuttle; Bacon Bum Brown, nicknamed for the fact that his rather over-sized rear end filled his short trousers to bursting point; Spotty Face Duncan, the Acne Kid; Stinker Smith, who never changed his socks or underwear unless his mother made him: Goofy Garbert, whose teeth were often used to open the bottles of pop they stole from Harry Gittens' paper shop; and last, but by no means least, Farter Foster, whose attempts at rectum recitals had made him a legend at Barnsford Primary. Here, having broken the unofficial record for the longest and loudest fart, he had single-handedly brought about the complete downfall of the history of the Roman Empire, causing Miss Marford, the history teacher, to report the whole of class D to Mr Bennion, and earning them a week of half hour detention during dinner time break.

Doug Bilbrook, the village bobby, knew the inside of their homes like his own, having visited their parents on numerous occasions. He was treated with utmost respect; a cup of tea and a piece of cake being the bribe that they hoped would keep their loved ones from behind bars.

No matter how often Billy and his men served doing time in their bedrooms, it could never cure the desire within to return to a life of transgression, giving concern to their parents that their offspring were heading for a life on the run. Which of course Doug Bilbrook knew they weren't, just lads being lads; but nevertheless a pain in the arse.

Billy had led his men into the most daring of raids, where they'd left their mark as swiftly and quietly as the SAS, fearing that being caught would result in a thick ear.

Old man Cleggy had woken one morning to discover that his prize-winning pedigree herd of Friesian cattle had been turned white over night, due to Alan Smith, his cowman, leaving the whitewash bucket out with a newly prepared load in it before going home the previous evening. Although he'd no real proof, Billy Jones and the Hole In The Hedge Gang were the first ones he thought of when reporting the affair to Doug Billbrook.

Harry Hapgood's ducks were let out each morning, whereby they'd make their way down to the stream that ran along the bottom meadow, always returning on their own in the late afternoon for a feed before being locked up for the night, safe from the clutches of old Raynor, the dog fox, or any other predators that might desire a bit of duckling for their supper.

So it was a worried Harry that went in search of them one day when they failed to return as usual.

There, bobbing up and down on the waters of the stream, were his twelve ducks; and a piece of string tied around each of their legs and then to the old willow tree that sat beside the bank was the reason for their failure to return.

"Them bloody kids! I'll have their guts fer garters when I catches 'em," promised a very irate Harry and, untying his grateful birds, led them back up the hill to the farm for supper, swearing above the sound of their quacking, and promising himself that he'd have the better of Billy Jones if it killed him.

Missions didn't always prove a success, like the time they tied a piece of fine cotton to Eric Cartwright's front door knocker, and while the other members of the gang watched at a safe distance from across the road, Billy hid in the bush by the side of the path, and pulled on the cotton to make the door knocker beat upon its base.

Eric, woken from a deep sleep, went to investigate who was there. Opening the door, he found that whoever it was had decided not to wait and gone. Billy hoped he would return inside, then he could repeat the prank again in order to get Eric's temper flaring. It had worked so often in the past with various members of the community that Billy looked upon it as one of his favourite tricks.

Eric, though, was in no hurry to go back inside. It was a beautiful evening, the stars were shining out of a pitch black sky, which to Eric presaged a frost. Having just woken up, he thought a bit of fresh air would revive him before his nightly trip to the Bowlers and, seeing he was outside, he might as well take the opportunity of relieving himself before returning to the house for a wash and shave.

Wandering over to the bush that Billy was hiding in, Eric unbuttoned his fly, and with a sigh of relief and satisfaction, peed all over the bush and its occupant.

Unluckily for poor Billy, it was a Saturday night, and being as Eric had had a dinner time session, his bladder was as full as a reservoir in springtime.

The lad felt the warm fluid pouring down over his head and the back of his neck, and although a slight move to the right would have saved him the discomfort of having it all over his face, he daren't move in case it caused the bush to rustle and reveal his presence to the fiery-tempered builder. For Eric wouldn't have bothered with the long arm of the law, but would have dealt out his own punishment, probably in the way of a clout around the ear and a kick up the arse.

Billy had been caught once before by Eric for letting his van tyre down, and although it only resulted in a glowing red ear that you could have cooked toast on, the way it had been executed, you'd have thought by the squealing involved that he was about to behead the lad.

After Eric had gone back indoors, Billy emerged from the hedge like a drowned rat, and much to the gang's amusement, gave the terrorising of the village a rest for the night and went on home for a bath. He told his parents, when they enquired as to what the smell was, that he'd fallen over in a pool of stagnant water while trying to rescue the Barnsford Boys' Five A Side football team's new leather case football from Pugh's Pit, after a badly taken penalty by Bacon Bum Brown. Having been the victims of the same lads' shot-on-goal the previous week while they were all playing in the field at the back of Bill's house (which caused the upstairs landing window to need replacing), his story held good stead with his long-suffering mother and father.

The day the gang decided to bunk off school for the afternoon, every detail was taken into consideration in order to give them a watertight alibi when interrogated the next day by Mr Bennion, the headmaster. Because interrogated they would be, and if they hadn't got a good enough excuse, then death row would have been a more pleasant alternative to the new cane Mr Bennion had invested in from the money raised by their parents at last month's parents' and teachers' cheese and wine evening.

During the late morning lesson, Billy had asked to go to the toilet, and while out of the classroom, he'd slipped out of the building, clambered up the drainpipe, and crept along the valley of the roof. Reaching the bell tower, he quietly tied the clapper of the school bell to the post of the tower so that when the headmaster attempted to ring it to call the children back to school after the meal time break was over, nothing would be heard except the quiet cursing of Geoff Bennion as he discovered that, for reasons beyond his understanding, he was unable to let his angelic little pupils know it was time to rejoin their teachers for afternoon lessons.

Returning to the classroom, Billy had to spend the rest of the Geography lesson cross-legged, owing to the fact that he'd been unable to get a pee in before he'd had to get back without making his absence appear suspicious. He was so relieved when his teacher had dismissed them for lunch, that, unable to hide his urge to empty his bladder, he jumped over his desk, and barging past the others trying to get there before him, bumped into

Mr Bennion in the corridor, where he received a lecture on running in the corridor, and pee'd himself in the process.

Having done the best he could to dry himself and hide the fact from his mates, Billy rejoined the gang outside the school gates and headed for Barnsford Mere.

Full of excitement and chattering like magpies as they went, The Hole In The Hedge Gang arrived at the Mere before the rest of their classmates had the time to unpack their lunches and go through the ritual moaning as to what would their mothers think they were playing at, by giving them such crass supplies to see them through the day.

Billy and his men had no time for food. They'd stock up their body fats later when they got home on sugar butties and such like. Now was a time for adventure and daring, a time for climbing trees and mischief. They had very little time before having to return for the final part of the day's learning, pretending that they'd lost all track of time through not hearing the school bell, or, if Bennion had decided to send out a search party, being discovered.

Climbing to the top of the two highest fir trees standing together, that grew alongside the waters-edge of the mere, Billy and Scar Face Bailey, began rocking them in an attempt to hit each other with the jumpers they'd taken off after reaching the summit.

These jumpers had been lovingly knitted

through the winter months by their mothers, with every line painstakingly checked for dropped stitches; and then, if one was discovered, undone and started again until, despite the sore fingers, there, behold, was a garment their child could wear with pride.

Whether it was the time they'd been made to spend holding the wool between their stretched-out hands as it was rolled by their mothers into balls, or the fact that the patterns had given them the appearance of Christmas parcels, here, at the top of the fir trees, they were being shown as much respect as a bag of rags.

The trees swung back and forth, creaking at the base until, fed up of that game, Billy and Scar face returned to the ground, unaware that there had been any danger whatsoever in what, in thirty years or so's time, would have made their hearts stop if they'd seen their own kids doing the same.

Now for the mere itself. There, lying on the shore, was an old punt that the Squire's gamekeeper had once used, to get out into the middle of this vast expanse of water and retrieve the water lilies that grew in abundance. Having done so, he would take them up to the Hall for Mrs Higgins, the housekeeper, who'd decorate the hallway with them.

Climbing on board the punt, the gang transformed into a crew of pirates, setting out to terrorise these treasure-laden waters.

Billy sat himself at the bow of the vessel, and

appointed Spotty Face Duncan, the more submissive of the gang, as the man to operate the pole to punt them out into deep waters. Then he barked out his orders to the rest of the crew as to what their roles were in this adventure, before lying back against the side, as though he'd been giving out such nautical commands all his life.

"Bacon Bum, you watch the shore fer the enemy; Stinker, you look over that side fer treasure. Scar Face, you look over the other side fer treasure; Goofy, open that bottle of Dandelion and Burdock."

"What about me?" enquired a rather hurt Farter Foster. "What shall I do?"

"Stick yer arse over the back of the boat and help Bacon Bum propel the ship," Billy quickly replied, sending the rest of his gang into a fit of laughter, upon which Farter Foster broke wind and joined in the fun.

The sun beat down on their heads as the craft made its way to the middle of the mere, making our weary sailors feel not only hot and sticky, but wishing they'd agreed to swimming lessons on Saturday mornings. Mr Bennion had enquired if anyone from class D was interested in making up a bus-load to go to Chesham baths, but seeing as none of them could as much as doggy paddle, the cool clear crystal waters of Barnsford Mere were as inaccessible to them as the Coral Reefs of the South Pacific.

"We're nearly in the middle," the Captain

hailed his crew, which inspired Spotty to give one last mighty push on the pole to get them there.

He pushed down with all his might, propelling the craft in the opposite direction but, as his hands slid up the pole to the top to grab it at the end, this time it remained upright in the water and his tiny digits slipped over the end, clutching at nothing but fresh air.

The pole had stuck in the mud at the bottom, which had sucked it out of Spotty's hands like a vacuum, leaving our band of pirates without a means of propulsion, stranded in the centre of Barnsford Mere, like a sailing ship with no wind.

Captain Billy didn't panic, but just calmly issued orders for the rest of the crew to dangle their hands in the water and paddle the vessel back to the pole in order to retrieve it. But to their horror, no sooner had these orders been issued, than the object toppled over and disappeared to the bottom of the mere.

"Dunner worry lads, we con paddle back t' shore," Billy assured them. "Spotty, yo an' Farter take that side; Brownie, yo an' Scar Face take t'other side and start paddling. Goofy, open that other bottle of pop, I'm bloody gasping."

Billy, who very rarely worked up a sweat unless it was in fun, was beginning to feel the pressure of leadership drying his throat, so sitting back in his place of command, he organised the steering of the punt while gulping far more than his fair share of the Cherryade which, along with the Dandelion and Burdock, had been purloined that very morning from Harry's.

The others, who always did as Billy told them to (partly out of respect for the fact that he was leader of the gang, and partly because of his left hand which could deliver a punch that had loosened a few teeth in the school yard before now), splashed about frantically in the water. But due to their trepidation at the prospect of spending the rest of their lives (what would be left of it without sweets and pop), marooned in the middle of Barnsford Mere, all they succeeded in doing was to spin the punt round like a fair ground ride.

Even Billy was beginning to loose his cool, shouting angrily at the others to cease messing about, and get the boat back on an even keel or, as he put it, "Stop pissing about an' git us back t' shore before we drown!"

After what must have been twenty minutes or so, the lads, so out of puff, and not having moved the punt a single foot, fell back into the craft completely exhausted, telling a complaining Billy that if he didn't discontinue his ranting, they'd cast him over the side and into the deep waters. Or, as a rather fed-up Bacon Bum Brown put it, electing himself as spokesman, "If thee dunner stop thee bawkin, we'll kick thee inta the bloody mere!" thus causing Billy to ponder his position as head of this band of cut-throats, whom he'd never before considered as mutineers. But now, as each man contemplated his destiny, the ugly face of revolt was staring him in the eyes, and he didn't particularly like what he saw, and shut up.

After about fifteen minutes of shouting for help, causing the boys to lose their voices, there followed an hour of complete silence, in which the only thing stopping the gallant pirates from crying was the presence of each other.

Billy sat there, the sun beating down upon his face, causing his lips to dry and become sore, and he contemplated his life, and all the naughty things he'd done, promising himself that if ever they got out of this alive, then he would change. Not like the promises he'd made to his mother on numerous occasions, never really intending to keep to them; this time he meant it.

Meanwhile, back at the school, Mr Bennion had been informed of the boys' disappearance, but owing to the fact that it wasn't the first time this very same batch of lads had gone missing without permission, he informed their class teacher not to worry, he'd deal with it in the morning, when (as he promised her that they would), the boys turned up for school as normal.

They were never really in any danger of being left to die of starvation, as the mere was used regularly in the late afternoons by the members of the Squire's workforce to do a spot of fishing before returning home for tea. And it was for that reason that Den Mullins, one of the Home Farm workers, spotted the punt with six little heads sticking up above the hull, marooned in the expanse of water like one of the lilies.

The lads all woke together at the sound of Den's voice hailing them, almost tipping the punt over.

"What you lot doing out there?" he enquired of the occupants, who he could identify as the dreaded Hole In The Hedge Gang from the red hair of their leader.

"HELP!" they all cried in unison.

"We've lost the pole an conner git back," Billy continued, once again resuming command, leaving the others to worry about their mutinous behaviour, and ponder on what form of punishment Billy would hand out in reprisal.

Den smiled at the thought of having the gang where everyone in the village would love them to be, and wondered what they would all give him to leave them there where they could be fed and watered until they all grew up and learned a bit of responsibility. But then he recalled his own youth, and how he too had been a pain in the arse to his fellow neighbours, and for that reason he smiled again and told the lads to hang on and he'd get the dingy from the boat house and row out and tow them in.

Mr Bennion flexed the new cane in his hands as the lads walked through the classroom door the following morning, having been informed by Mr Harding, the school caretaker, as to the reason for the school bell's silence the previous day, and dealt out the punishment to each in turn.

"Six of the best."

***Doug, who'd brought the dog into this world, had
decided that he was the only one to set her free...***

CHAPTER ELEVEN

OLD BESS

Doug Youd gave old Bess a gentle pat on the head and promised her that if she was feeling better that evening, then he'd take her with him to The Bowlers for a drop of beer, or, if she was really up to it, rabbiting.

Looking up at her master, the old dog gave a sharp bark, partially out of love for Doug, but mostly from the pain she was in. Then, pulling herself up from the blanket that she'd slept on for the past fourteen years, she climbed out of her basket. Struggling to walk, she staggered across the stone kitchen floor, where she gently licked the back of her master's outstretched hand as he pulled on his worn-out wellington boots, still smelling of cow muck from cleaning out the heifers the day before.

Trying not to let his wife see the beads of tears that were forming in the corner of his eyes, Doug gave her a kiss and left for work.

Cycling along the road to Thompson's farm where he worked, it seemed strange not having Bess running along side him, her ears pinned back in anticipation of how many mice she'd catch that day as Doug began his daily routine by organising the cattle feed in the mealhouse.

Doug began to recall the first time he'd seen his old dog, one of Jim Rutter's Jack Russell terrier bitch, Kim's, litter of six. In fact, she was the smallest; hardly alive when Doug, who was always called upon to aid in the birth of the villagers' pups, helped a struggling Kim to deliver her.

"I dunner think that uns goin t' make it," Jim told Doug, looking over his shoulder. "Her looks rit sickly."

"Well, if her does make it, put her down fer me. I like a fighter," Doug informed his mate, as he pushed a straw down her throat and breathed into her the first breath of life, causing the pup to give a little sneeze before being laid alongside her mum for warmth.

Saying his goodnights to the Rutter family, he mounted the rusty old cycle that was leaning against the wall by the garden gate, and rode home to inform the wife that there'd soon be the patter of tiny feet in the cottage.

Six weeks later, after numerous visits to monitor the pup's progress, the day arrived for Doug to go and pick her up.

He was like a child as he set off to the Rutter's place. It had been over ten years since he'd had a dog, Penny. He and his wife had sworn, despite their love for the creatures, that they would never be able to replace her, and they didn't want to go through the pain of losing another.

Elsie had never been able to have children, so Penny had been the substitute, receiving all the love and affection they would have laid upon a child. So when she went, the Youd's had been so distressed by her demise that they vowed they would never have another one.

For ten years they kept that promise, always declining when offered a pup or mature dog by one of their neighbours. They'd even had to endure blackmail, when someone would beg Doug to have one of the litter he'd just delivered, or would tell them about a dog that had lost its owner, or had to be found a new home for some reason or other to save it from being put down.

So it came as a surprise when Jim Rutter only mentioned, in conversation to Doug in the Bowlers one night, that his Jack Russell bitch was having another litter and he was on the lookout for prospective buyers.

"When they due?" Doug asked.

"Why, thinking of 'avin one?" Jim enquired, only really joking with Doug, and never expecting him to say yes.

"Aye, I might be," Doug answered and, downing his pint, bade Jim farewell, and told him to let him know when they were born.

That night, Doug got home from the pub, and after telling Elsie about his conversation in The Bowlers, he was delighted when his wife said that she would love another dog to keep them company.

"Besides," she pulled her husband's leg, "it'll give me summit t' talk to when thee's asleep in the chair."

So with both agreeable, it was just a matter of picking the one they wanted.

"Yo con do that," Elsie told her husband, when they discussed it. "After all, it'll be going t' work with you, so yer'd better make the right choice; we dunner want one that'll cause havoc at the farm and git up Mr Thompson's nose."

Bess cried all through the very first night she was brought home, and it took a lot of will power on behalf of Doug and Elsie to stop them from going down into the kitchen and bringing the pup to bed. But persevere they did, and within the first week Bess was sleeping through the night in her basket in the kitchen.

It seemed no time at all before Bess the pup had grown into Bess the fully-developed dog, and although still like a puppy at heart, it was time to begin the training that would enable her to take her rightful place by her master's side down at the farm.

Bess learnt quickly, and within her first year had become an obedient servant to Doug without losing any of her own character, which would never have been broken, as Doug found out, even if he'd spent twenty four hours a day trying to correct.

Doug and dog went everywhere together; work,

fishing, rabbiting, the Bowlers; even when Doug went for a game of Bowls on the little green behind the pub, Bess would sit at the side of the green and watch her master. Her head cocked from side to side as he chased after the round pieces of wood that rolled along the surface. When she had first seen them, she had given chase. This had earned her the disapproving scoldings of the Home players, or meant that she had to evade the flying feet of the less patient Away team.

Doug and Bess were a couple, and when out on his own, the first thing anyone enquired of him, before asking about Elsie, was, how was Bess and why wasn't she with him?

Elsie didn't seem to mind her back seat role and, although having to put up most of the time with playing second fiddle, she loved the dog as much as Doug did, nursing Bess on her lap in front of the fire whenever Doug had to go out without her.

A rabbit ran across the road in front of him, and Doug, watching the white fluffy tail of the small rodent vanish into the hedgerow, thought of how Bess loved to chase them, never knowing when to give up. Many a time Doug had had to return home for his shovel to dig her out of some burrow she'd got herself stuck down.

He remembered the time she went missing when, after a week had passed, Doug and Elsie had given up hope of ever seeing her again' assuming, despite scouring the countryside for her, that she'd got stuck down some hole and died of starvation.

Doug was inconsolable, coming home at night from his searches and just sitting in his chair by the fire stroking his leg where the dog would have lain.

Ten days she was missing, and then one morning Doug awoke to the sound of Bess whining and scratching at the back door. Leaping out of bed, he raced down the stairs two steps at a time, and upon opening the back door, he was greeted by a sight that caused a lump to reach his throat.

Bess sat there looking up at him, pride written all over her face, and between her front paws, snuffling and snorting, and trying the best they could to crawl under their mother's belly, were four of the cutest pups Doug had ever seen.

Doug felt a little embarrassed, for this expert at dog midwifery hadn't even noticed that his own canine companion was in pup, never mind the fact that she'd decided to have her pups without the help of her master. But quickly overcoming his embarrassment, he shouted upstairs for Elsie to come and look what the stork had brought.

The pups stayed with them for over two months, before all being found homes that Doug had vetted himself. And although Bess never had any more, the mothering instinct remained with her all her life, always finding time to play with one of their neighbour's pups when out walking with her master.

Looking over the hedgerows at the freshly mown hayfields that littered the countryside, Doug recalled the time he'd taken Bess harvesting with him, and she'd gotten herself a little tied up in her excitement.

It was a beautiful early June evening, and Doug, who'd been in the hayfield all day turning the grass with Mr Thompson's rickety old turner, had returned with the baler to turn the now yellowing grass into oblong blocks of forage, neatly held together by two lengths of bale string. They were thrown out of the back of the implement for the men behind with the tractor and flat trailer to load and take back to the farm for stacking. There they would stand, ready for use when the winter months made it impossible for the cattle to go out into the fields and graze the pastures.

Bess was running to and fro with her nose firmly fixed to the ground, picking up the scents of rabbits who'd earlier been playing about amongst the rows of neatly turned hay.

Unaware of anything around her, Bess never noticed the bailer, and before she'd had time to get out of its way, it had scooped her up and eaten her whole.

Doug had been turning round looking to see if the men were catching him up with the loader, and not being aware of Bess's dilemma, carried on up the rows of waiting grass.

It wasn't until he turned around again to take another look at the others' progress, that he noticed his dog's head protruding from one of the bales of hay.

Stopping the tractor, Doug jumped down and ran as fast as his legs would carry him to where his pet was entrapped, where on his arrival, Bess let out a sympathetic yelp in the hope that her master would set her free.

Doug cut the strings that tied the bundle together, parting the layers of hay, not knowing what cuts or broken bones she'd suffered, and reached in and picked his dog up.

By some miracle, Bess didn't even have a scratch on her. Somehow (and Doug couldn't imagine how), she'd evaded the blades and spikes that were part of the works of the machine and passed through without any harm.

Bess took more care of what was going on around her after that, and although her nose was still always firmly planted next to the ground, she always had one eye cocked in anticipation of any dangers.

Doug came home from work that night, and instead of plonking himself down at the table in expectation of his tea, took his shotgun from the hook on the wall, and calling Bess, informed his wife he was taking her out for a spot of rabbiting as promised.

Bess once more struggled out of her basket and quietly followed her master out of the back door and down the garden path, through the old wicket gate and into the field at the back of Doug's cottage.

Bess was slow, pain showing in every step she took, but her eyes lit up at the prospect of being out once again with her master, and she tried as best she could to stay to heel.

Elsie only heard one retort from the gun, and assumed, when she heard her husband's return, that it had been too much for the old girl, and they'd returned to share the fire together.

Elsie heard the grating of her husband's boots on the gravel path, and through the kitchen window near where she was doing her ironing, she could see her husband come around the corner of the house and go into the shed, returning with his spade. Bess, who was never far from her master, couldn't be seen.

Elsie sat in the old chair by the fire and waited for her husband to come in.

After about fifteen minutes, Doug entered the door and, hardly able to look his wife in the face, dropped to his knees by the side of her chair, placed his head on her lap, and cried like a baby.

"Bess's gone," he said, and Elsie, who knew the pain he was in, just rubbed his thinning hair, and tried to hold back her own tears.

Doug, who'd brought the dog into this world, had decided that he was the only one to set her free, and doing the kindest and yet the hardest thing any master could ever do, had saved his beloved Bess any more suffering.

They never had any more dogs after that, but Doug still delivered the pups of the village, always thinking of Bess whenever there was a runt, and always doing his best to see that it made it through.

Bess was never far from Doug and Elsie's thoughts, and the picture of her that stood on the mantelpiece was a reminder of the joy she'd brought into their lives.

"Have yer never seen owt like that before?" Gus asked, trying to milk every ounce of fun he could from the situation.

CHAPTER TWELVE

THE YANK

"Just passin' through, boy," Mervin would holler in his loud, ear-piercing Texan drawl when anyone inquired about his business within the district.

"Just takin' in the sights of your beautiful little country."

Little; that was the term he used to describe everything, from the views he'd seen in London to the creatures that grazed the fields around the village of Barnsford.

"I love ya little cows, so cute and cuddly, make ours back home seem so big."

"Say, what little tractors ya have around here. Ah bet ya could drive over the top of them with ours, and not even knock the stack off."

"Ya know, these little cars of yours take some getting' use to. Ah keep thinkin' I'm driving a dodgem."

Gus Devenport, whose own twenty-eight stone frame had been likened to Mervin's sixteen year old nephew's (who, according to Mervin, still had another five years growing left), was the only one who didn't get upset when anything he owned was put down by the American as a prop from Gulliver's Travels. Instead, the wily old farmer would just slap the American on the back, knocking every ounce of breath out of his lungs and give him a sarcastic reply, which had the others tittering in their beer but went clean over this colonial cousin's head.

"How big's ya farm, Gus?" Mervin asked the old farmer one night.

"About seventy acres," Gus answered.

"Well, ma uncle's got a ranch back home in Texas, that when ah wanner drive across it in ma car, ah have to set of at dawn in order to get to the other side by nightfall."

"Aye, I knows what yer mean," said Gus, smiling at his neighbours over the rim of his glass of bitter. "I had a car like that once."

And, downing his pint, placed it along side the American's empty whisky glass in order to let Mervin show how generous the folk from the New World were.

It was the sixth pint Mervin had bought his three drinking pals that evening; Gus, Bob Black and Eric Cartwright had all apologized for not having the resources on them to reciprocate the gesture. This was owing to the fact that they should have only slipped into The Bowlers for a quick half before bedtime. Still, it never dawned on Mervin that he was being exploited by these so-called haysticks, and he was only to keen to dip his hands into his trouser pockets and show what wealth could be earned in the Land of the Free.

"Ah guess you folks don't earn that much, serving a little community like this, ah mean."

To which they all agreed and downed their latest pint and placed the glasses back on the bar for yet another refill.

That Saturday was the Barnsford Horticultural Show held, as always, in the main hall of the primary school.

For the past twelve months now the men of the village had nurtured their plots of land, sown their seeds and fed their prize fruits, vegetables and flowers as though they were helpless little babies. Now, this forthcoming Saturday, was their chance to prove to the neighbours, that when it came to growing onions, tomatoes, carrots, etc, then the secrets handed down from father to son over generations, were the reason that various mantlepieces and sideboards of homes throughout the community were covered year after year in silverware.

On the morning of the show, Joe Bright turned up for work at seven o'clock as usual. As ever, Gus Devenport was sitting there waiting at the bottom of the drive, with the cheeks of his huge backside spread across the milk churn stand, marking time for Joe to arrive so that he could tie his boot laces.

Gus trusted no one else; since he was twenty-eight stone in weight and hadn't seen his feet for a good many years, it was important to this colossus of a man that he should not be brought tumbling to the ground by something as trivial as a loose boot lace. This he knew would never happen if Joe tied them, as he could tie knots and bows that would turn the most experienced mariner green with envy.

"Joe," Gus whispered into his farmhand's ear, "when tha's done that, I want thee t' go down t' bottom field, an' bring me back the biggest ox cabbage tha con find."

"Aye, alrit boss, but wot does thee want with an ox cabbage? I thought thee wer only entering yer beans this year."

"Never yo mind, just do as I ask, and make sure yer in the Bowlers at dinner time."

Joe returned to the farm hardly able to carry the vegetable, and after plonking it down on the table in the scullery, he fell backwards into one of the great beech chairs that surrounded the old pine table, in the expectation of Mrs Clark (the Devenports' housekeeper), pouring him out a reviving mug of tea.

Gus's boots grated on the stone scullery floor as he dragged his weight into the room and took up the whole area in front of the fireplace, in order to warm his huge bum in front of the fire, causing Joe to feel such a drop in temperature that a shiver ran through his body as if someone had just walked on his grave.

"Eh lad, that's a beauty. Just what I wanted,"

Gus congratulated Joe on his choice, and with that picked it off the table and took it out to the outhouse to find a sack to put it in.

Come 'knocking off time', Joe did as he was told and went to The Bowlers for a dinner time pint, before going home to get washed, changed, and pick up his own home-grown produce to take along to the school hall to show.

Mervin was already at the bar just having downed a whisky, and as Joe ordered his pint and went and sat down waiting for the arrival of his boss, Mervin continued to try and impress the rest of the hangers-on by once more getting in the beers.

It wasn't long before Gus made his entrance, dumping the sack on the bar next to Mervin, and then standing back and waiting for the American to play his part and get him a drink.

"A pint for Gus and the lads and another scotch for me please, John."

Then, turning to face the huge farmer, Mervin played right into his hands and enquired as to what was in the bag.

Gus dipped his mighty hands into the sack, and with the theatrics of a Shakespearian actor, brought out the ox cabbage, and held it out in front of Mervin as if it were the skull of a giant Yorik.

"What in darnation's that?" Mervin gasped.

"It's me entrance fer the show," Gus replied, seeming to glow with pride.

"I gathered that, but what is it?" As once again

Mervin tried to fathom out what Gus was entering.

"Have yer never seen owt like that before?" Gus asked, trying to milk every ounce of fun he could from the situation.

"I guess not," Mervin had to admit, a little despondent that the old country couldn't match this with anything he'd ever seen.

"Well," Gus began to tell him, turning slightly sideward to wink at his pals, "it's a Brussels sprout, an yer wunner find any better in all the world!"

Eamond, the landlord from Hell, had made his mark.
One night into the job and he'd upset the entire male
population of Barnsford.

CHAPTER THIRTEEN

THE LANDLORD FROM HELL

"Time please, Let's 'ave yer glasses."

Eric Cartwright took his father's old chain watch from his waistcoat pocket and glanced at it for the second time in less than a minute. The last time he had been pondering over where old Gus was tonight, and if there was still chance he'd pop in, but this time it was to check that it hadn't stopped.

He also looked at the clock behind the bar for the second time. The last time was to check if his was right, which he did by extracting ten minutes from the time shown on the old railway station clock (which had been that advanced in time ever since John and Doreen Wilson had taken over the place); this time it was to check that the pub clock hadn't mysteriously increased by an extra fifty minutes.

No; both timepieces gave the same information; it was twenty to eleven, time for at least another hour's drinking which, in Eric's estimation meant at least another four pints, and a couple more whiskies.

"Come on, please, I won't tell yer again. I'll just take yer glasses," came the second command, causing the clientele of The Bowlers Arms to almost choke on the beer that was at that moment lubricating their tonsils.

Even Doug Billbrook, local constable of the parish, couldn't believe his ears, thinking that this intrusion to his night off must be some kind of practical joke organised by John and Doreen before they'd set off on their hols.

It had only been two hours ago since the regulars had been introduced by John to the stand-in landlord, and quarter of an hour later they had been standing outside the pub waving their hosts off on a well-deserved two week break on the island of Majorca.

In fact, Betty (the local haulage contractor Alan Perkins' wife), would be on her way back home right now, after taxiing them to the airport. She would be quite alarmed if she arrived back to the house to find Alan already back from The Bowlers, and still sober.

"This is yer last chance to sup up, yer've been warned," came what seemed like the final threat.

"What's up with yer, man? There's plenty of time yet," Eric expostulated, wondering as to whether this man had ever done the job before. But before he'd had time to ask the question, the chap had thrown the bar towels over the pumps and turned over half the pub lights off, just leaving enough glow for everyone to see themselves out.

"He comes highly recommended," Doreen had informed the lads, when they'd asked about the nature of the stand-in pint puller a few nights earlier.

"Apparently he ran the Royal Oak at Tilbury last year, and they said he'd done a marvellous job."

"Well, as long as he dunner give us any mither, we wunner give 'im any," old Gus assured a rather nervous Doreen and, winking at the rest of his cronies in his usual mischievous manner, continued to inform her that he'd be made very welcome.

If only old Gus was here now, thought Eric, I'm sure he wouldn't be feeling so bloody hospitable to the bugger. And with that, he slammed his pint pot down on the bar like a child, and stormed out into the warm September night air, muttering and cursing under his breath. Although the remaining customers had a little chuckle at Eric's childish behaviour, it was only a matter of seconds before they were following him out the door with a flea in their ears after being accused of having no homes to go to.

Eamond, the landlord from Hell, had made his mark. One night into the job and he'd upset the entire male population of Barnsford. Even those who'd not attended his opening night had heard enough, from those who had, to despise this man beyond any loathsome creature that walked God's earth. This did more for the Bowlers' takings the following night than any stay back, due to the fact that people turned up in their droves to take a close look at this monstrosity the breweries had provided.

Some tried to make polite conversation with the man, whereby in return all they got was a one-word reply or a snort of air from his rather large proboscis, causing the long hairs that hung from the nostrils to whistle like a wind in a wood.

Some tried to be smart and put him down with their sarcasm, only to be rebuffed by the fact that he didn't even seem to notice it.

Gus, on hearing about this challenge from a very indignant Eric Cartwright, made every effort to attend, and he tried to use the best of his repertoire to lure the prey into committing the act of being made a fool of, but to no avail. Eamon just grunted, pulled pints, and generally got up everyone's nose, up until ten forty. When, just as the night before, he called time, placed the towels on the pumps and turned down the lights, infuriating them even more by barging his way around the pub, picking up the glasses the moment they became empty. He even took a few from the customers' hands as the last drops of beer were being savoured.

"Summit's got t' be done about the bugger," Eric confronted Gus.

"Aye, but we dunner want t' spoil John an' Doreen's holiday by coming back t' any mither."

One of the villagers wasn't so considerate, so when Eamond woke the next morning and went out into the car park to let the Wilson's dog relieve itself, he discovered his car covered in cow muck and a note informing 'the stand-in' of the fact that he was making their life hell, and if he didn't behave he'd receive more of the same, only not so well versed as that.

Obviously this crude and rather offensive letter had not been signed, but from the state of the handwriting and spelling, it was clear to the recipient that it hadn't come from anyone who sat in the snug.

Even Doreen's pet sheltie had taken a dislike to its stand-in keeper. So much so, that on the fourth day of Eamon's visit, cries of help from the bar window alerted Mrs Cooper, who happened to be passing on her way to clean at Doctor Killshaw's house, that someone was in dire need of rescuing within the licensed premises.

She summoned up help in the form of the newsagent Harry Gittins, and they managed to find their way in via the back door, and were able to rescue Eamond from the fiery little dog by coaxing it into the kitchen with the promise of food.

Eamond climbed down from the stool he'd taken refuge upon, instead of showing his thanks by the way of offering them a drink (a usual form of gratuity offered to a person in the way of appreciation by a publican), he nodded his head and grunted something that resembled a thank you, before showing them to the door and ushering them out into what had turned into a rather wet and blustery morning.

William had taken such a dislike to his miserable keeper that the night The Bowlers was burgled, he never even uttered a whimper in the way of letting Eamond know he was in danger, probably hoping that the landlord would be murdered in his bed.

The burglar came in via the small opening in the top of the bar window, a gap that ruled out most of the regulars, owing to the fact that the majority would have trouble getting their arms through, let alone their huge girths.

The only thing taken of any value was the new payphone John had recently installed, saving him a great deal of money, having in the past had to let his regulars use his own phone to ring home with their varying excuses as to why they'd be late home for tea, or call out local taxi driver Mike Morris, to transport them home. But, as William had chewed the one in the house during another disagreement with Eamond, it left The Bowlers without any communication whatsoever with the outside world.

The fortnight passed, with Eamond becoming more unpopular each night, until the evening arrived for John and Doreen's long-awaited return.

Once again Alan Perkins wife, Betty, had driven to the airport to meet the Wilsons off the plane and bring them home. Once again, Alan settled himself down with his cronies in the bar of The Bowlers for their return, feeling pretty content that this was Eamon's last night, and therefore would almost certainly mean - with the return of John and Doreen due before closing time - that a late night lock-in could be anticipated and enjoyed by all.

The plane was delayed that night due to some technical problem, and closing time came around without any sign of the drinkers' saviours.

"Last orders!" came the shout from the bar.

The orders came thick and fast from all over the bar as the hardened drinkers got in their provisions in case John and Doreen were delayed past the drinking-up time.

"Three pints of brown mix, please."

"Two pints of bitter and a double whiskey."

"Three bitters."

"Put us another half in there and draw us another two pints."

For they were determined that this was a night for celebration, and the end of their partial prohibition.

Eamond gave them until quarter to eleven, five minutes more than on any other night (proving that he did have a heart), and then, as if he were programmed to continue his duties to the end, he started.

"Time gentlemen, sup up and let's be 'avin yer glasses."

By eleven o'clock, everyone was so sick of hearing his voice that they'd submitted to his demands, drunk up and handed in their glasses; all, that is, except Alan Perkins.

"Come on, Alan, drink up and let's be 'avin yer on yer way home," Eamond said to the wagon driver, as if he were a child.

"I'm waiting fer the missus," Alan protested, confirming the landlord's theories.

"Well, wait outside then so I can clear up and get t' bed."

"But her's bringing John and Doreen 'ome from the airport," Alan tried to reason with the barman.

"That's not my problem. I'm not paid t' keep the place open longer than ten forty, and seeing as it's now five past eleven, I'm telling yer to go home," and with that he swept Alan's remaining full pint off the bar and tipped it down the sink.

Alan's face turned red with anger, and those who'd remained to see the outcome of this act of defiance suddenly surrounded the fiery little driver, telling him that it wasn't worth the bother, and tomorrow he'd be gone and out of their lives for ever.

Alan snatched his jacket off the peg by the door, ripping the collar as he did, bidding Eamond good night and, telling him that if he never saw him again it would be too soon, walked out of the door and off home.

It was about a quarter of an hour later when the back door to the pub opened up and in walked John, Doreen and Betty.

"Where is everyone?" Doreen enquired,

amazed to find the place like The Marie Celeste.

"Eamon's probably chucked them out." Betty thought she ought to let the publicans in on the goings-on over the last two weeks. She hadn't mentioned a word on the subject on the way from the airport, not wanting to put a damper on what had appeared, by their chatter, to have been a very enjoyable holiday.

"Well, where's Alan?" Doreen continued to pry.

"Probably at home by now."

"Well, ring him up an' tell him t' get back round here for a drink with us." Doreen had made her mind up. She wasn't going to let the matter stop there.

"I can't," Betty replied sheepishly, having again saved her friends the shock of knowing their home had been robbed during their absence.

"Why?" Doreen pleaded.

"Because you don't possess a phone."

Eamond left the following morning, with no one there to wave him off; not even the Wilsons came out to say goodbye, having hardly spoken a word over breakfast. But as his car made its way past the pond and out of the village, John put his arm around his wife as they stood at the pub window, watching to make sure no harm came to the man in the way of a lynch mob.

"Well, one good thing'll come from this," he told Doreen. "We should be appreciated a little more for a few months at least."

*"Now, rads, I want you to sing the words crearry
and precisery."*

CHAPTER FOURTEEN

LARRY LLOYD

"Harrow, rads."

"Morning, Mr Lloyd."

"Rooks rike rain rater."

"Aye, but dunner yo worry, we'll soon have the roof on."

"Werr, I'r reave yer arone fer a rittre whire, whire yer sort yer gear out, and I'r go and make you orr a cup of tea."

Larry Lloyd could easily have held the title of the nicest man in Barnsford, if not the world, with never a wrong word to say about anyone (well, except for the pronunciation). Nothing, if it was in his power, was too much trouble when anyone asked for his services in any way.

What held Larry in everyone's affections, even more than his good deeds, was the fact that he couldn't pronounce his L's properly, sounding every L as an R. What made him such an endearing character to his friends and neighbours alike, was that he never shirked from using them. In fact, he probably used more words with L's in than anyone else on earth which, on occasion rendered his listening public helpless, as they tried the best they could to hide the humour they were being exposed to, as Larry endeavoured to captivate his audience with ripping yarns of riveting context.

Everyone's favourite was the story of the man with the wooden leg which, despite his telling over and over again, always had his audience in stitches, causing Larry to believe that this must rate as the funniest joke in the history of comedy.

Even more comical to everyone was that Mrs Lloyd had the misfortune to have been christened Emma, so whenever she was introduced by her husband to anyone who had never made her acquaintance before, he made a special point of letting them know she was his spouse, by introducing her as:

"And this is the good rady, Emma Rroyd," - an introduction that caused this timid and easily embarrassed woman a good deal of discomfort. Still, she was always too much a lady to contradict him, and for all the humiliation it must have caused her, she loved her husband dearly.

Larry was a clerk of the works with the local highways department, and it was his job to see that the lanes around Barnsford were always in good order, which, considering he couldn't even pronounce the word, were a credit to his dedication to a job he loved as much as life itself.

But the most remarkable thing of all was that Larry loved to sing. So much so, that when the post came up, Larry applied for the job of choirmaster at Barnsford church. Seeing that no one else had put their name forward, the church committee had no other option but to grant him the job.

Barnsford's claim to fame as the music centre of the world was a very insignificant one indeed; in fact, when it came to a musical ear, Barnsfordites were generally tone deaf.

Doreen Wilson, the landlady of The Bowlers Arms, had been playing her piano two keys out of tune for as long as she'd been there, accompanied by a drunken Eric Cartwright each and every Saturday night, mimicking a banjo with the bed warming pan that hung on the lounge wall. He heartily sang out his limited repertoire of 'In Dublin's fair city', and 'I belong to Glasgow', accompanied by Doreen's dog howling like a demented wolf. To any passer-by, the awful noise that came from the place would have sent shivers down their spine.

Even so, the regulars of the congregation dreaded the thought of visitors to their Sunday services (or anyone who'd paid out good money to hire the choir for weddings), having to listen to the Lord being praised with exclamations of 'Harrerujah praise to the Rord' from twelve angelic-looking school boys dressed in their fine white tunics; or to know that the primary school would now have 'Jeruserem' as the title of their school hymn.

"Now, rads, I want you to sing the words crearry and precisery."

"What's he say?" Johnny Dodd asked the boy next to him.

"He wants us to sing the words clearly and precisely," answered Tony Bond from the back.

"Now, heads back and take in rots of air into your rungs."

"What's he on about now?" another of the bemused youngsters asked.

"Lots of air into our lungs," once again came the explanation from young Tony, who seemed to be able to understand what Larry was saying, and relate it to the others. He had become an interpreter for the rest of the choir.

Slowly, with the aid of young master Bond and their ability to change r's back to l's, the young sopranos came to terms with their teacher's speech impediment, and before long, instructor and instructed were in unison with one another. So when their first public performance was heard, despite everyone's fears, the choir sang like a host of angels, word-perfect, and each word clear and as audible as anything produced by the Vienna Boys' Choir.

It would have been nice to think that while in the service of the Lord, Larry would have been the recipient of one of his miracles. He wasn't, and continued to greet the men working on his home with: "Harrow, rads," each morning as though it were the natural way to talk.

As for Mrs Lloyd, well, she put up with the embarrassment with as brave a face as could be expected from someone who would always be introduced by her husband (albeit in complete innocence), as a pain in the arse!

At the official enquiry there was never any proof to tie the fire in with the Squire...

CHAPTER FIFTEEN

THE PRESERVATION ORDER

"Bloody hell! The old bugger's up to his tricks again!"

The air filled with the pitiful cry of one of Chesham Council's planning officers, waving a piece of expensive notepaper in the direction of his office companions. He gestured with the forefinger of his other hand at an offending letter he had just received. The others stopped their flicking of rubber bands at each other, and turned to see the cause of this sudden woeful outburst.

"Who?" came the muffled enquiry of one, as a mouthful of egg and cress sandwich his wife had lovingly packed for his lunch (and which had now been devoured along with the other five before he'd hardly had time to work up an appetite), came spurting out of his mouth and all over his neatly-written letter of application for the new post he was seeking in Transport. Although the query had been aimed at confirming his already keen suspicion, he had a sneaking feeling about what everyone within the planning department of the Chesham Council Offices already knew.

"Bloody Squire Barnsford only wants to knock down an entire listed farmhouse to make way for a galvanized cattle shelter," continued the luckless member of staff. Unfortunately the letter had been placed upon his desk, meaning that from now on he'd have to be the one to deal with the awkward old aristocrat, a commission for which he held no great relish at all.

Simon Walker's grave news was only met with sniggers from the others, who, having run out of rubber bands, continued to do battle by flicking paper clips at each other. The transport applicant finished off the remains of his wife's efforts to give nourishment to this hard-working servant of the rate-paying public, and briefly carried on gazing dreamily out of the council office window at the young lasses making their way along the street opposite in the direction of Chesham County High. In truth, this was the one reason for this enthusiastic Local Government Official turning in before the allotted clocking on time of nine o'clock. His attention was again brought back to the work place by a badly typed screwed-up letter of apology to Gus Devenport flying through the air. The crumpled-up ball of paper was an attempt to tell the farmer that his plans for a large monstrosity of a pig pen had been rejected, and it hit young Mr Walker on the head, once more causing cheers to echo around the office, along with cries of; "Good luck old boy," and, "It's not too late to put in for the transfer to the Sanitation department," (a proposition that at this moment looked really tempting to the unfortunate Civil Servant).

This wasn't the first time Simon Walker had dealt with Squire Barnsford. Only six months ago, not long after his arrival from Education, he'd been given the chance to clash horns with the Squire over a galvanized tin roof that had been erected on one of his workers' cottages. Although he had been keen and ready to take on what he'd described to his new colleagues as, "a toffee-nosed old fart", the memory of that encounter still caused a great deal of embarrassment whenever he recollected the moment, especially as he drove past the cottage on his way to work, or was reminded by the rest of the department whenever the Squire's name should crop up during the everyday proceedings of the Chesham Borough Council Planning Offices. It was no contest, the Squire just went ahead and erected it. And although the case was still officially being dealt with, he had less chance of getting the Squire to change the roof than he had of persuading his wife to let him buy the Triumph motor-cycle he'd been offered by young Simpson over in Accounts.

Simon's sickly smile at the rest as they continued their banter couldn't hide the disappointment he felt at once again being the one who'd fallen foul of the Squire's desire to reshape the appearance of the surrounding countryside. But even now, with him once again in line for the butt of all the others' merciless humour, the thought of a victory and revenge against the council's strongest adversary, gave Simon the ability to take on this task with an alertness that would hopefully bring him the conquest which would put him right up there with Sir Malcolm Harper, whose portrait hung in the main hallway of the County Offices. A man who'd risen to fame over half a century before when he'd taken on the Squire's father, and beaten him in the case of the Barnsford village pond. A victory that, even though no one could remember anything about it (other than its title), had made him a living legend, and had probably even won him the respect of King George. The monarch had never liked the Barnsfords, ever since he'd been made to go there as a child and spend his holidays fighting daily with the present Squire's father over everything from who sat where for breakfast, to who would win the heart of young Sally Rowlands, the gamekeeper's daughter; which was the reason for Mr Harper's Knighthood only months after the story of the Squire's defeat had reached the King's ears.

Yes, Simon told himself, this time it would be different, this time he knew what he was up against. Bring on the Squire, and let them all cease their laughter, for now he'd show them what he was really made of.

Simon's highly polished Ford Anglia jerked its way up the drive of Bolthrope farm, with its driver not knowing whether it was the bumpy surface or the prospect of his encounter with the Squire that was making him feel rather nauseous. What ever the reason, he only hoped he wouldn't spoil his chance of creating an impression of authority to his opponent by throwing up all over his adversary's brogue shoes.

As his car came to a halt, and the young County Official stepped from the confines of his motor vehicle, there waiting, propping himself up by his stag's horn walking stick (and looking as though another helping of Mrs Higgins', the Squire's housekeeper's, fine cooked English breakfast would have snapped the piece of brier in two), was the portly figure of the Squire dressed in his usual checked jacket, trousers and waistcoat.

"M-m-m-morning, W-W-Walker. I hope Y-y-ou had a pleasant j-j-j-journey?" the Squire enquired, stammering in his usual overbearing manner.

"Y-y-y es, th-thanks," came back the reply, causing Simon to turn crimson at the speech impediment he'd just acquired.

The Squire was not offended by what would have seemed to most as mimicry, as many a subject seeking an audience with his Lordship had suddenly found themselves floundering for words, as the overwhelming demeanour of this landed gentleman gave the impression that he was about to pass sentence upon them.

"Well, l-l-let me explain what I'd l-l-l-like to do with the place," and the Squire related his plans before Simon had been given the chance to tell him that he'd already seen his proposals for the building, and that he would have to convey his apologies on behalf of the Planning Department, but permission would not be allowed. Simon waited to tell him that it had been refused because to raze this grand building to the ground in order to erect what could only be described as 'an affront to the wishes of those who felt very strongly about the conservation of such wonderful constructions of architecture such as this', but he was cut short when a slate came tumbling from the roof of the dilapidated old farm house, and crashed with a metallic clatter on the roof of his pride and joy, putting a dent in the bodywork - as well as the hope of an outright victory over the Squire.

"Oh my God, look at my car!" squealed the official, almost bursting into tears at the realisation of what this encounter was going to cost him in the pocket, as well as the irreparable damage to his sanity.

"Y-y-yes, that's the r-r-reason we need to kn-n-nock it down," pointed out the Squire. "C-c-could cause some harm one day."

"It already has!" screamed Simon, beginning to forget that he was here to save the place, and now wishing that it had never been built.

"That's going to cost me a bloody fortune to have put right," he exclaimed, and with that he attempted to wipe the fragment of the slate off his roof, causing more damage in the way of scratches, as the rough edges of the offending projectile scraped its way across the paintwork.

"W-w-well, do you agree it needs to c-c-come down?" the Squire inquired with all the sensitivity of a bull elephant.

"Right now, I couldn't care less if you put a stick of dynamite under it and blew it up, but unfortunately I have to inform you that, as a listed building, you are not allowed to alter or deface the exterior in any way."

"G-g-good God, man, the bloody thing's falling down around us. It's full of dry rot, damp rot, woodworm, and I-I-I w-w-wouldn't be surprised if, if we continued this argument at a few decibels higher, the damn thing didn't come c-c-crashing down in front of our very eyes."

And with that, the Squire hollered out, "Fall, you b-b-b-bastard!" before turning his back on Simon and heading back to his estate car. Due to the old man's confidence in this so called 'national asset', he had had the sense to park a good distance away from anything capable of doing the same damage as it had to the chap who was preventing him from rendering it safe from killing anyone.

On the way back to Chesham, Simon had to make a couple of other calls; a garden shed that had been put up without the consent of the neighbour, a wall that had been rebuilt using an extra thousand or so bricks, thus claiming land that had not been within its boundaries before.

Everyday problems that to Simon were part and parcel of working within the Department of Planning. But as he neared the outskirts of Chesham, he had to stop to let three fire engines dash past in the opposite direction, making him take evasive action so as not to receive any more damage to his already impaired motor.

"They seem in a hurry," he told himself. "Must be a big blaze somewhere," and with that he once more pulled back onto the road to complete his journey.

As he walked back into the office, everyone began the cheering again, but despite their childish banter and nearly having his eye put out by a paper aeroplane, Simon was feeling quite proud of himself. He had just scored a historical victory over the Squire, and the news must by now have reached the ears of those who worked alongside him. Jealousy would be eating their insides out.

"Well, you showed him," came a cry from the far corner, and with that everyone began to howl with laughter.

"Who supplied the matches?" came the taunting call of another.

Simon looked puzzled, and after being asked by Spriggs if the Squire had offered him a bribe, he demanded to know the meaning of these remarks.

"What the bloody hell are you on about?" he asked.

"Bolthrope Farm. It's on fire. Billy's just come

back from the fire department, and they've just had a call from a neighbour to say the place is well ablaze."

At the official enquiry there was never any proof to tie the fire in with the Squire, but rumours spread when Mrs Jenkins had informed Mrs Rider in the butcher's shop one day that John Hughes had been talking to Tommy Roden, who in turn had heard Jack Longsdale telling Arthur Price, that Ben Whitehouse had heard somewhere, that the Squire had been seen leaving the scene of the crime with an empty tin of petrol. Although they weren't sure it was petrol, and they couldn't really say whether or not it was the Squire (as they'd been at least three fields away) and after all, with all the smoke, well, they weren't 'definite enough to say fer sure like.'

His mother tried the best she could to keep him entertained, by reading to him, playing games such as scrabble, snakes and ladders...

CHAPTER SIXTEEN

THE BARNSFORD BULLET

The breeze blowing through the open window stirred the curtains in Bobby's bedroom and caused them to move slightly to one side. So, from the confines of his bed, the lad could tell by the deepening colour of the sky and the sound of a lone blackbird sitting high up in the old silver birch at the end of the garden, singing out a frantic warning to batten down the hatches; a thunder storm was imminent.

Bobby had lain in this position for the last six months and, having witnessed the many changing moods of Mother Nature through the twelve panes of glass that formed his window, he always hated the aches and pains thunder storms created in his motionless little legs. Limbs that had once carried him with such a pace across the football field that they'd made him the scourge of every team's defence in the Chesham and District Primary School League.

It was now approaching the end of July and, with the summer passing by so fast, Bobby had come to accept that, this year at least, he was never going to enjoy the long warm days that came to make a small boy's life seem that it was going to be like this for ever. And that growing up and becoming an adult was something that happened to parents, or the spotty-faced youths who hung around the pond at night, revving their motor-cycles to the point of nearly blowing their engines up, and making such fools of themselves, as they tried the best they could to win the attentions of soppy girls.

A tear ran down his cheek as he thought of his mates out playing. Six weeks of school holidays ahead of them, and nothing to do all day but kick a ball around, wander the fields and woods (occasionally calling at the village shop for supplies of pop, crisps, pear drops and the like). If that all became a bit too tedious, there were always the trips to the Blacksmith's shop, or 'Dangerous Dave's' to relieve the boredom.

Bobby did get visits from his pals who, letting him in on all the news and what they'd been up to, caused him to laugh, but in reality only added to his deepening depression when they left, as he sullenly reflected on the fun he was missing out on.

His mother tried the best she could to keep him entertained, by reading to him, playing games such as scrabble, snakes and ladders, and, if time allowed, monopoly (of which usually both participants became bored before anyone ever had the chance to win outright). Unfortunately she had her own jobs to attend to; cleaning the house, preparing the meals, washing, ironing, and trips to the shop; and when alone, the house echoed to the silence of only his own company, and this made Bobby feel even more depressed than ever.

"Hello, John. Come for our Bobby?"

"Aye. Is 'e in?"

"Just this minute got up, lazy bugger," and with that Bobby's best mate John Farrel and Bobby's mother laughed, as Bobby put his uncombed and bedraggled head round the corner of the kitchen door. Sleep was still clogging the corner of his screwed-up eyes, and a white line ran down from the freckle-covered left side of his mouth where he'd slobbered during his dream-filled slumber.

Bobby lifted the spoon from the bowl of cereal he held in his other hand, and waited until he'd crammed the contents into his mouth before greeting his mate with a spray of milk, cornflakes, and a muffled, "How do?"

"Bobby," his mother chastised him, "what have I told you about speaking with your mouth full?" and with that, Bobby and his young friend both burst out in a fit of giggles, causing more milk and bits of chewed-up cornflakes to splatter out of Bobby's mouth and on to the hall carpet. This earned the culprit a hearty clack behind the head from his annoyed mother, which only had the effect of causing more of the lad's breakfast to end up all over the floor as he spluttered once more. Bobby tried desperately to regain his breath after nearly choking on a free gift that he'd failed to notice drop into his dish as he'd hurriedly poured the contents from the big cardboard box.

As Bobby's mother scurried off into the kitchen to fetch a floor cloth, the two buddies went through into the front room, where breakfast could be finished off more calmly in front of the television, and plans could be made for the rest of the day.

"We'll take the sledge up to the Long Fields; it's better up there than on the Church hill," Bobby insisted, hoping his friend would agree, and not get cold feet like last time. Not surprising, though, after witnessing Bobby's failed attempt at trying to leap the hedge at the bottom of the field - via the hump in the run made by old Brock the badger. He'd already watched his mad mate pulling all the thorns out of his hide, and had refused to be persuaded to better the endeavour.

Dragging the once brightly painted red sleigh that Bobby's father had made two winters ago out in the shed at the back of the house, the two lads pulled it down the driveway and out into the lane that led towards their destination, much to John's dismay, Long Fields.

It had snowed again in the night, so as they walked they kept turning to gaze at the imprints their Wellington boots, and the runners of the sleigh, had made in the soft fresh covering. The blinding snow had once again carpeted their village, giving it a look of total serenity, and it somehow muffled the sounds that gave away the existence there of any form of human occupation.

Bobby broke the silence. "I'll jump that hedge t'day," he muttered.

John, not sure whether he was addressing him, or just trying to convince himself that it was within his capability to risk his life again in the hope of having something to brag about at school on Monday, pretended not to hear. He just shoved his hands further into his pockets for warmth, and dragged his feet in the snow, which instead of crisp imprints, now gave the impression to any would-be tracker that one of the team was badly injured, and was having to be dragged to whatever destination they were headed for.

When they reached the brow of the hill from the village side, they both gave a gasp of wonderment as they gazed down the long smooth surface of the toboggan run, only blotted by that same hump of ground just in front of the hedge at the bottom.

"Who's going first?" Bobby asked, knowing full well that, due to his friend's reluctance to be posthumously awarded any medals for bravery, it was sure to be himself.

"You can," John replied, without hesitation, feeling pretty sure that by the time his friend had smashed the sleigh beyond any form of makeshift repair, he'd be saved the embarrassment of being labelled a chicken.

Bobby positioned the sledge on the very crest of the steep and treacherous downhill run and, having paused a few seconds to decide whether to make a sitting or lying-down descent, dropped onto his belly on top of the now fading red wooden 'Barnsford Bullet'. It had been aptly christened this name in the back garden shed, after his father had just added the second coat of bright gloss, and had turned to both his son and friend, claiming with all the pride of any of the great mechanical engineers, "This should go like a bullet, lad."

One big gasp for courage, then Bobby shouted his command to his assistant to give a big push and launch him on his way.

John's hands were too cold, and he couldn't be bothered to get them out of his duffle-coat pocket, so, placing his foot against the wooden framework between his pal's legs, he gave it a quick shove and let the hill do the rest of the work.

Within seconds of the launch, the Bullet was up to speed, with the twin blades of its runners cutting through the snow like a couple of knives. Bobby's fingers gripped the edge of the sledge like a vice, and, although he could hardly feel them (because the cold had extracted any sense of feeling from those tiny skin-covered bones), they still managed to create an imprint in the top layer of paint, as the adrenalin caused every muscle in his body to tighten. It was as if he had developed suction pads as his whole being seemed to cling to the surface of his sledge; his knees, toes, and even his chin were now gripping onto the Bullet as it gathered speed with every yard it travelled.

The journey seemed endless, time having no meaning as the blur of the snow-covered field passed him by. What should have been fun had now turned into terror, as the hump of Brock's lair grew closer and closer.

John just stood open-mouthed as he watched with a mixture of admiration and pity for his friend as he sped down the hill to what seemed like certain death, knowing he would be the only witness to what lay ahead.

He didn't even blink, but stood there mesmerised as the sledge suddenly changed course from a downwards trek, to aiming skywards, as it hit the ramp and flew through the air like a fighter plane.

It was only in John's sight for a matter of seconds, but as it cut through the early morning atmosphere, the sun's rays seemed to flash off the metal blades as they skimmed the top of the hedge, knocking the snow from the branches of the hawthorn as they passed over. Then suddenly it disappeared. Only a scream, and a puff of white powder rising from the field beyond replaced what had been a most amazing sight - and then silence.

John stood there, rooted to the ground as his legs became paralysed. For what seemed like an eternity, the only visible sign of anything having taken place that morning on Long Field were the twin tracks of the Barnsford Bullet and a patch of green hedge, the width of a small sledge, which had been cut out from the mound of snow on either side; and directly in line with the tracks was old Brock's residential entrance. Bobby had done it, but at what price?

John remained motionless, staring at the scene of Bobby's triumph, too afraid to call out or run down the hill to see what had become of his pal. If only they'd gone to Church Bank like he'd wanted to. If only it had rained instead of snowed last night. If only Bobby wasn't so bloody stupid. If only. If only. John kept thinking of all the probabilities that could have resulted in his friend still being in one piece, and all the time he thought, not a sign of the gallant test pilot could be seen from his viewpoint on the hill.

After what seemed an eternity, John plucked up the courage to walk towards the disaster scene, slipping and sliding down the side of the hill like a duck on a frozen pond. With all fear now vanquished, all he could think of was getting to the other side of the hedge as fast as he could, hoping that he wasn't too late to do something to help Bobby.

Peering through the gap the sledge had made in the pile of snow that lay on the top of the hedge, John didn't know what to expect. He certainly didn't anticipate finding the corpse of his friend having been snatched from the scene of the accident before it had hardly had time to go cold.

The sledge lay about five yards into the next field. The wood that held the right-hand side runner was completely smashed. Just beyond that was the imprint of what could only have been made by the face-down body of the pilot. Then, John noticed the footprints leading away from the crash site, and following them with his eyes along the hedgerow, noticed they disappeared into the ditch and out of sight.

As he tried to lean over the hedge to get a better view, he felt something grab the back of his collar and the seat of his pants and, before he had time to react, he was toppling head first over the hedge and into the next field.

Looking up over his forehead from his cumbersome position on the ground, John could see the impish smile of Bobby as he peered down at him from the Long field side of the hawthorn hedge, and it was then that John had wished that Bobby had broken his bloody neck.

Bobby laughed, John just scowled and then threatened to knock his head off when he got hold of him. But within minutes they were both pulling the now crippled sledge home, at the same time slapping each other on the back and marvelling at how well the Bullet had performed, and wondering whether Bobby's dad would be able to mend it before the next fall of snow.

Monday morning, Bobby was at school and, as John predicted, spent most of the morning boasting about his exploits on the Bullet.

Tuesday, Bobby woke up feeling a bit under the weather, but seeing as today was football, he managed to drag himself to school with the hope of scoring another three goals like last week.

Come dinner time, he was feeling so poorly that his teacher took him home, and upon hearing from Miss Williamson about his inability to take part in the day's activities, his mother ordered young Bobby to bed and went across the road to the phone box to ring Doctor Killshaw.

The doctor diagnosed flu, and gave instructions for the lad to remain in bed. Upon leaving, he handed his mother a prescription, and told her to pick it up from the chemist in Chesham. Then he left, with the reassurance that he'd pop in the next day to see how the lad was faring.

The next morning, not long after his father had left for work, Bobby, needing to answer the call of nature, left his warm bed and very slowly made his way to the bathroom on very shaky legs. It wasn't until the return journey that Bobby's legs gave way altogether, and he was left helpless on the bathroom floor.

Bobby cried out for his mother, and within seconds of his calls being heard, she was cradling his head in her arms, trying to comfort her distressed son. Later that morning, Bobby was on his way to Chesham Infirmary in the back of an ambulance.

*   *   *

That was over six months ago, and now the fearless pilot of The Barnsford Bullet was still lying in bed unable to move his legs.

It wasn't the crash that had caused this immobility, but Rheumatic Fever, brought about by a minute bacteria, rendering our hero helpless. Although a full recovery was finally made, thunder storms and balmy nights still cause Bobby's legs to ache, bringing back memories of that winter of 67, and the last flight of the Barnsford Bullet.

It was said that Tom's language would have made Lucifer himself blush...

CHAPTER SEVENTEEN

FOOLS BEWARE

Tom Rutter hadn't always been a farmer, although farming ran throughout every vein in his body, and there wasn't a season of the farming calendar which held any mystery to the man.

His father had taken over Yew Tree Farm from Tom's Grandad; likewise he'd taken over from his father and so on, for probably as long as there had stood a farm on that part of the land.

No, Tom had left home at the age of sixteen and joined the army at the start of the First World War. As if that hadn't been enough, he remained there until the outbreak of the Second World War, where, from the rank of Sergeant Major, he once again took on the might of the German army.

But at the end of his second campaign at the age of forty-seven, he decided that he'd had enough adventure for one lifetime, and retired to take on the challenge of battling with the elements and help his ageing father with the running of the farm.

Now, at the age of seventy-six, nine years after most men had retired, and two years older than his father had been when he died, he was still fighting. Never taking fools lightly, and never shirking from a strong word when needed, he feared no one.

It was said that Tom's language would have made Lucifer himself blush, and, never stopping to consider the company he was in, he filled the air with clouds of blue vocabulary whenever vexed. Which, due to his very short tolerance of anyone and everyone, was a regular occurrence and, unfortunately for his long-suffering wife, didn't make them the first choice in couples when invitations where handed out for various social gatherings of the farming folk of Barnsford.

But despite his explosive nature, Tom never held grudges, and it wouldn't be long after giving his opponent the full bombardment of his artillery, he'd be offering his usually defeated adversary a peace oblation in the way of a rolled cigarette, a clout on the back, and a way of making good the situation by allowing them to buy him a pint the next time they met in The Bowlers.

As an employee of Tom's, Sid Mathews had been the butt of most of this foul and abusive language for twenty-three years, ever since taking up the post of farm labourer for Tom on his retirement from the forces.

Sid was only twenty-two then, the same age as Tom's own son Jackie and, being small, was the target of Jackie's cruel and aggressive behaviour, brought about by the need to take it out on someone for the verbal bashing his hard-to-please father gave him.

Jackie would show off mercilessly in front of the older members of the workforce by picking on Sid from the moment he arrived on the farm. That was until he offered Sid a chance to put on the gloves and do a bit of sparring with him. Sid, who, unbeknown to Jackie, had boxed for years at the Chesham boxing club, gave the upstart a thrashing he'd never forget. Seeing as it was during a dinner time break, and the rest of the labour force were all looking on as Jackie had hoped to impress them with his pugilistic skills, the boss's son had no choice than to accept defeat gracefully, and admit he'd been beaten by the better man.

From that day on, Sid and Jackie formed a bond that, try as they might, no one could sever. Not even Jackie's father who, sometimes wishing he'd never set eyes on the pair of them, was incited to increase the contents of his own vocabulary to words that he'd never dreamt of using.

Not long after taking over the reins from his father, Tom was offered the chance by the Milk Marketing Board to let them do surveys on his milk yield, in order to make sure he was able to command the best prices for the product.

"What we need for you to do, Mr Rutter, in order that we can keep our records intact, is make sure that all your beasts are named and recorded," Mr Twist of the board informed the farmer; and although intimidated by the sheer size and demeanour of Rutter's presence, he still managed to keep an air of authority as he issued the instructions as to what was and was not expected of him.

"As long as it dunner interfere with me day t' day running of the bloody place, I'll git one of the lads t' git vicar up 'ere and we'll pissin' well christen the buggers as well if yer bloody like!"

With that, Tom Rutter turned his back on the official and left the scene to go for his breakfast, a meal from which the delicious bouquet was now floating out of the kitchen window and across the yard, causing the mouths of all that it engulfed to water.

That night, Tom walked into the shippon as usual, just to do his final round of the place before issuing the men their orders for the following morning and retiring to the big house to set about his tea - yet again, a meal that you could march an entire army on.

Peering along the dimly-lit building, and through the steam given off by the sweaty cows, Tom could make out Sid and Jackie about half way down the shippon, standing next to a large black and white Friesian cow heavily in calf, both scratching their heads and peering down at a note pad held in Jackie's hand.

Tom noticed that the milking hadn't even started, and the cattle were getting restless, kicking and swishing their tails in boredom.

"What the f*"/!?g h*ll's going on?" Tom hollered at the top of his voice, causing not only the two men to stand as if to attention, but the cattle as well.

"We're trying to give them all names," Jackie tried to explain nervously to his father, "but we seem to be running out of ideas."

Tom took one menacing step nearer, almost filling the walk-way and blocking out any means of escape for the now terrified farm hands, who knew by the colour of their boss's face, and the way the veins were now standing out on his neck, that an explosion of not too pleasant wordstock was about to spew forth from the volcanic opening in his face.

"Call them f*"/!?g p*ss, f*"/t, s*!t and a*!eh*!e for all I f*"/!?g care, and then just get on with the f*"/!?g milking!" and with that Tom did an about-turn and stormed out of the building and across the yard to the house, cursing and swearing as he went.

Soon after, a poor lorry driver from a bagged fertilizer company felt the wrath of the big man.

A month previously, Tom had ordered a wagon-load of fertiliser to be delivered to the farm in the spring, which being another three months off, would give him time to pay off his already large amount of debt, and therefore have the money to pay for the goods without having to resort to credit.

Then one day, while Tom was at market, the load arrived ahead of schedule, and the driver painstakingly carried every bag into a place at the far end of the storage shed, where it now stood neatly stacked along side the few remaining bags from the previous year.

Just as the driver was getting Sid to sign for the load, as the farm hand didn't know that it wasn't supposed to be arriving for another eight weeks, Tom's big black Rover car pulled into the yard, and, blocking the path of the lorry, came to a halt almost bumper to bumper.

"What the f*/k are yo' doing 'ere?" Tom curtly enquired.

"I've just delivered the fertilizer yer ordered," the driver responded, feeling the blood rushing to his face as if in readiness for the confrontation about to begin.

"Well, yer con just f*"/!?g undeliver it. I never asked fer it t' be delivered until the spring."

"B-but I've just carried the whole bloody load into the back shed on me own," the driver pleaded.

"Aye, an yer con put it all f*"/!?g back on the lorry on yer own," and turning menacingly in the direction of the already quickly-disappearing workforce of his own, "'as these lazy buggers 'ave gotten jobs of their f*"/!?g own to do." And before the driver could continue to plead for leniency, Tom Rutter had about-turned and was now heading in the direction of the house in order that he could give his wife a verbal lashing over the unpaid bills for last month's market. Which, unfortunately for her, had caused her spouse a great deal of embarrassment when challenged over them, especially as he'd been bawling out the market manager at the time over his unwillingness to let Tom uprate his credit.

Now, the years having passed by, Tom's temper, instead of mellowing in his old age, had finely tuned itself to the point, that no matter how good a day he'd had, it only needed a slight prod in the right direction and it were as if the gates to hell itself had been opened.

After one gusty night, Tom was greeted by the news that a large old oak had toppled in Top Field, and, having ripped up its roots, it had fallen across the main road leading to Chesham.

Tom was rather pleased with the news, for, being so old, it had been a threat for years. Only too glad it had come down without injuring anyone, the old man could only think now of the plentiful firewood it would supply for the coming winter months.

"Get the bloody chain saw from the shed," Tom instructed Jackie. "We'll have the bugger cut up in no time, and while yer think on, open up the f"*'/!g gates at both ends of the field, then any bugger that wants t' get passed, con drive across the bleeding field and be on his f*"/'!g way."

All morning Jackie and Sid cut away at the tree, trying the best they could, under the old man's supervision, to get it into reasonable enough sizes which would be possible to man-handle onto the trailer that was hitched behind the David Brown tractor.

Tom took it upon himself to direct the traffic across the two fields that enabled them to drive in through one gate, and out of the other further up the road, and therefore be on their way, usually with a polite 'thank you' to the farmer for his consideration of their need to be about their business.

It was almost dinner time, and the oak was now in a position where it could be hauled to one side in order to clear the road, when around the bend, further back towards the village, the squealing of car tyres broke the silence which had now fallen with the switching off of the chain saw.

A rather large and important-looking Humber car suddenly shuddered to a halt just in front of where Tom was perching on a nice dry cut log, sending up sawdust all over the farmer and causing him to topple backwards off his seat as he sneezed.

Tom stood up, wiping away the sawdust from his eyes and nose. He noticed the pennant on the front of the car, which proclaimed it to be an army vehicle, and meant that, to the trained eye (and having been in the military as long as Tom had, his was as trained as you'd get), it was obviously carrying some member of the top brass.

Tom was about to wander over to the driver's window and give the culprit a piece of his mind, when all of a sudden the back driver's side window was wound down.

A small dainty head, wearing an officer's cap which covered a neatly tied-up bun of hair, popped out of the opening, and before the farmer had time to open his mouth, a strict and rather well-spoken female voice addressed Tom as though he were a school boy.

"I say, you there, can we get past? We are rather in a hurry, you know."

Sid and Jackie slipped back behind the protection of the mighty oak, as they could see the swelling already beginning to take place in Tom's neck.

"Well, you'll just 'ave t' bloody well wait, wunner thee," the old man informed a startled-looking listener. "When me men 'as loaded that there tree onto that bloody trailer, which by the looks of the time is going t' be after dinner now, then tha'll be able t' be on tha way."

With that, Tom turned his back on the woman and began instructing the men to pack up for lunch.

"I say," the woman began again, "what if we were to drive through your field like that van's doing? pointing in the direction of Tom Stanworth's butcher's van as it drove through the first gate across the fields and out back onto the road, with a wave of greeting from the driver to the farmer, and likewise an acknowledgement back from the old man.

"No, yer can't," Tom retorted.

"Why ever not?" questioned the determined lady officer.

"Because that's my pissin' land and I f*'"!/g say

not," Tom continued his stubbornness, resorting to stronger language as he became more agitated by this woman's arrogance.

It was obvious to the bystander that this lady could be as persistent as ever Tom Rutter was; something to do with the army training, Sid thought; but there was no way that she could ever be allowed to have the last word. So when she finally played her last card, by addressing the driver in a manner that everyone else within earshot could hear, "Really, and to think that our boys fought for the likes of this during the war!" it brought steam bellowing from Tom's ears, and a riposte that caused the entire cast of this drawn-out saga to blush with embarrassment.

"Listen, missus, I was f*"/!?g fighting fer this f*"/!?g country when your f*"/!?g c*"t was as f*"/!?g big as a f*"/!?g shirt button. Now either f*"/!?g wait till we've 'ad 'r f*"/!?g dinner and moved the f*"/!?g tree, or turn round, f*"k off, and find some f*"/!?g other way t' git past."

And with that, the farmer shut the gate, and producing a lock (which he got out of the Land Rover he'd driven to the job in), put it on the gate, got into the vehicle and drove off. A missile of sawdust was sent in through the car window, causing the lady officer to splutter and spit for all her worth, as he headed back in the direction of the farm, and his dinner.

Now, not only Harry, but many of his neighbours sat in their armchairs with tears in their eyes, as they pondered their future...

CHAPTER EIGHTEEN

THE PLAGUE

The Squire stood at his bedroom window and gazed down at his legacy. In the daylight hours, it would have spread before him like a quilted rug. Now, with the cloak of darkness having spread itself upon the land, the electric light of hundreds of sixty watt lamps twinkled from the occupied domiciles of his subjects, as they either sat before their television sets eating their evening meals, or, having finished, had washed and dried the dishes, and were talking about the day's events and how it was effecting their lives.

Although the obscurity of a late Autumn evening had enveloped most of the vista, the parameters of these little hamlets were illuminated by the huge bonfires that were spread as far as the eye could see; silhouetting the trees, telegraph poles, or any other inert form that didn't have to cower with fear from the ghoul that now walked the land, as they stood like guards between flames and Barnsford Hall.

The Squire, not able to stand the obnoxious smell of burning flesh and smouldering bones any longer as it was carried by the winds to infiltrate his domain, reached forward and pulled down the sash window, shutting out the mid-November air and the pungent pollution it carried on its back.

It was only a couple of months ago he was congratulating Harry Craddock on his award for the 'Best Bull' in show, at the Chesham Country Fair.

As the ruddy-faced chubby little old farmer stood there, proudly clutching his red rosette and polishing his cup with spit and the worn sleeve of his jacket, the Squire had asked him if it were possible to use the great bovine in the siring of his own herd.

"De-p-pending on p-p-price, of course," the Squire had stuttered, partially because of his impediment, and partially because the need to discuss payment always brought out the worst of his affliction.

All that was now left of that fine majestic beast was the ashes of a two-day-old fire, dug into a pit and covered in lime, where, along with the rest of Harry's herd, it was no longer a cause of concern for the men from the ministry, whose task now was to help the farmer scrub down his byres and shippons in the hope of eradicating the spores of any disease that remained.

Harry's had been the first in that area to fall foul, and now, two weeks later, the bonfires were raging throughout the length and breadth of the countryside, as if Guy Fawkes was being honoured every night of the week. Now, not only Harry, but many of his neighbours sat in their armchairs with tears in their eyes, as they pondered their future and recalled the hours of toil and sweat in the building of their precious stock. Visions of their cattle waiting in turn for the ministry guns to put an end to their lives were still fresh in their minds.

You didn't have to be a farmer to be affected by this terrible disease, nor did you have to be remotely connected with the farming community. Just simply the fact that you lived or travelled throughout the rural area was enough to include you in the restrictions that had now been enforced within the community.

All social gatherings, football matches, dances, youth club, scouts and girl-guide meetings, had been cancelled in order that contamination through any form of gathering could be kept to a minimum. Even The Bowlers was suffering, with farmers and farm labourers avoiding contact with one another, for fear that they might be the one responsible for passing the malady on.

During the daylight hours, all that could be heard was the noise of earth-digging equipment, as more pits were dug to dispose of the corpses; the lowing of the now fast-disappearing cattle (who seemed to sense the disaster that had come to Barnsford); and the sound of gunshot as every form of vermin was desperately being eradicated from the area, in the hope that this would lessen the chances of the plague being spread.

Nothing was given reprieve; jackdaws, magpies, jays, and rooks were blasted from the sky without mercy, their limp bodies gathered and burnt. Although all hunting had been cancelled, any hope the foxes had of being left alone was cut short as they were ruthlessly flushed out and shot, destroying more in a matter of days than would be lost in many seasons of the more traditional way.

School continued, but many farmers' children, whose parents' farms had not yet caught the disease, were kept at home in the hope that none fraternisation with their class-mates would reduce the chances of contamination.

And although no one dreamt of curtailing the word of the Lord, the Reverend Bunting's congregation was down to a mere half-a-dozen or so. All those absent were missing some of the vicar's best works, as his sermons laid blame for the plague on Man's lack of commitment to the church (a slight reference to the fact that the church roof restoration fund was a couple of hundred pounds down on the expected amount hoped for at this stage in its development).

All Harry Gittin's delivery boys had been laid off, meaning that anyone wanting a paper had to risk bumping into some other members of the community in the newsagent's, but having taken that risk, usually found themselves buying extras in the way of cigarettes, confectionery or magazines to read during their confinement to quarters. This gave Harry the idea that it might be a good long term business plan to completely dispense with the services of his lads, but he reconsidered when he pondered on how many only bought the paper to read the sport, and if it meant getting out of bed early on a Sunday morning, they probably wouldn't bother with one at all.

Yes, the plague had taken hold of the land, or, as it was more commonly known, 'Foot and Mouth'; and now it was the job of the Agricultural Ministry, the police, the vets, the farmers, and all those who lived within walking distance of any form of cloven-hoofed creature, to try their best to pull together and destroy it.

There'd been reports of outbreaks down south, but Harry never gave it a thought when, on his morning inspection of the herd as they came in from the fields for milking, he'd noticed one of the prize milkers hobbling a bit. Thinking that it was nothing but a sprain, he decided to wait until after milking before giving Mr Harris, the vet, a ring to request a call in order to give her a good looking-at.

Mr Harris looked up from his crouched-over position and, as he let the foot of the animal drop back to the ground, shook his head in despair. He never spoke, but pulled himself upright and forced open the beast's mouth, inspecting the sores that had developed on its tongue and back of the throat.

"It's not good news I'm afraid, Harry." Mr Harris placed his hand on the farmer's shoulder to comfort him. "I'll have to get confirmation, but

I'm positive it's Foot and Mouth."

"What do I do now?" Harry enquired solemnly.

"Get yer beasts inside, place some disinfected straw down at the bottom of the drive and a bucket with disinfectant in it, and deter any coming and going from the farm. In the meantime, I'll inform the Ministry and we'll take it from there."

The vet removed as many of his garments as he could and placed them in an old plastic fertilizer bag, washed his hands in the disinfected water that Harry had brought from the kitchen in a bowl, then left the farm to inform the Ministry and the police.

Looking back at the figure of the farmer through the driving mirror, Mr Harris could make out the slumped shoulders of a man he always admired for his posture, and he realised there and then that this wouldn't be the last time he would be announcing the same diagnosis to one of these hard-working, God-fearing custodians of the countryside. It would only be a matter of time before he would be getting his next frantic telephone call to confirm what the farmer would already know in his heart to be the disease.

Diagnoses were made, the authorities were informed, cattle were destroyed, burnt and buried. Buildings were scrubbed clean, and all the time the farming community held its breath, awaiting the day when they'd receive the all clear, when they could restock. Or, if they'd been lucky enough to avoid the disease, sell their cattle at the re-opened markets, which had stood closed and deserted throughout the crisis. Or not have to wake each day with the fear that they were the next victim.

The farmers who'd lost their cattle were remunerated by the Government, who paid well to enable the re-stocking of herds, but that didn't compensate for the years it had taken in rearing a prize-winning lineage of their own; beasts they could proudly parade around the show ring at the County Fair, or watch as the bids went up and up for a young heifer they'd been responsible in raising.

The plague finally left the land, but its scar remained etched upon the pastures of Britain, like the hollows in the face of someone who'd suffered from chicken pox.

Harry Craddock picked his pipe up off the mantelpiece, which embellished roaring flames that licked the back of the fireplace, and placed it into his mouth. Not bothering to light it, but just sucking on it as if it were a dummy, the way many of these men did when they hadn't time, or were too deep in thought to ignite the tobacco that lay in its bowl. And as he did, he gazed misty-eyed at the photograph of himself standing next to his prize-winning bull, cup and rosette proudly held in front of him, with the creature snorting defiantly at the camera man. And he knew that it would be the duty of his son now, barely twenty-two years of age, begotten late in Harry's life and still learning the ropes, to produce the next 'Best of Show'.

Squire Barnsford came over to George... and explained the fundamental rules of pheasant shooting.

CHAPTER NINETEEN

THE COUNTRY GENT

George Rigby was the epitome of the self-made man. Starting off with one old broken-down lorry he'd bought with a loan from his wife's Uncle Jack, he'd worked all the hours God sent until he now owned a fleet of haulage trucks. The livery was so well known, they could be recognized wherever they went trundling along on any road in the country.

With a back-up staff that filled a large office over his depot in Chesham, a manager who was intent on trying to please George in the hope of being made a director, George now decided to relinquish the reins and settle into semi-retirement.

So when he noticed in the Chesham Herald that Byron House (the home of the recently departed Lady Mary Jones Robinson, sister to the Bishop of Chesham), was up for auction, George made sure he was at the front of the bidders in Barnsford village hall, determined to outbid anyone; as the thought of making it into the upper echelon of the landed gentry did more for his ego than the thousands that lay earning him interest in the bank.

The bidding quickly rose to seventy thousand pounds, but as the bidders dropped out one by one, George kept on winking his runny eye at the auctioneer until finally, at what many considered to be a ridiculous price, George clinched the purchase, and became the proud owner for eighty-two thousand pounds. Which, although it made a considerable hole in his bank balance, was nowhere near what he'd been prepared to pay for the privilege of becoming a country Squire, thus leaving him plenty of scope for bringing in the architects, builders, interior designers and decorators to renovate the place to his and Mavis, his wife's, liking.

George had walls knocked down, then built new ones and discovered fireplaces and doorways that no one even knew existed. He installed oak beams and panelling, modernized the kitchen, and turned the cellar into a replica of his favourite bar room at The Crown in Chesham. He built a games room consisting of full-sized snooker table, bar billiards table and dart board, converted the bathroom into a modern-day version of a Roman baths. But his greatest accomplishment was the Gothic style hall and stairway, with its sheer size and ostentatious decor taking away the breath of anyone who entered.

George had money, and therefore wanted everyone to recognize that he did by making sure everything he bought was expensive. But, unfortunately, neither he nor his wife had taste.

What could have become the elegant country home of a hard-working retired businessman, was turned into an onyx and gilt framed French Chateau, with great hideous works of art, huge gaudy coloured drapes, over elaborate and totally out-of-character furnishings, and a colour scheme that would have made a pot-smoking flower powered hippy feel nauseous.

That was inside. Outside was something else. Old established shrubs were torn up without mercy, rose bushes were ripped out of the ground while still in bloom, the herb and vegetable gardens were ransacked, the herbaceous borders (which Lady Mary had painstakingly restored to their former glory), were dug up and thrown on the heap with the rest of flora. In their place appeared a Gazebo, an ornamental carp pool, patios covered with huge pots and statues of Greek Gods. There was a tarmac tennis court, a heated outdoor swimming pool, and fountains that gushed jets of water into the air, before falling back to earth, splashing and spraying into huge stone bowls where Mermaids sat lazily around, bathing their tails in the spume that formed on the surface of the pea-green coloured liquid.

The five-bar gate that had stood precariously hanging on one hinge at the bottom of the drive (creating a groove in the ground where it had to be dragged back and forth as it was opened and shut), was replaced by two elegant wrought iron ones, depicting peacocks and the name of the elaborate residence. These could be opened and shut remotely from the main house, by means of giving your name to who ever answered your call from the phone in the box at the side, or, if you were the resident, by the remote control gizmo carried in the vehicle. Something that, due to the fact that he could never remember to change its batteries, often led to George and his good lady having to climb the wall, walk through the grounds to the house, and then open the gates manually by the controls situated discreetly in a little cupboard in the hallway.

The peacocks on the gate were complemented by six real ones within the grounds. These were allowed to wander freely around the gardens, often escaping, upon which George would have to bring them back from some irate neighbour who had been woken earlier than they'd have liked, by the mating calls of the amorous cocks as they roamed the countryside in search of a hen. Something George had failed to provide them with due to the fact that they weren't flamboyant enough to go with the settings.

George took to smoking large cigars and, in the evening, drinking brandy, a change from the woodbines and beer he'd always been used to. Although he enjoyed his visits to The Bowlers, where, even though he managed to Lord it over what he now considered 'the working classes', he would always find himself in awe of Major Bantam.

After a while he took to frequenting Warmington Grange, where, despite the regular clientele's disgust at his back-slapping whenever he was in their presence, or the farting and belching as the rich food he was now consuming took a grip of his digestive system, he tried his utmost to impress and become accepted.

George bought himself a horse, a broken-down old nag called Bunty, which, if it hadn't been for the fact that George knew nothing about horses but didn't want to admit as much by taking someone along with him who had any experience at these matters, would probably have ended up at the knackers' yard.

After a few lessons at a local riding school, George decided it was time to apply for membership of Sir William Walker's Hunt. Whereby, thanks to his wonderful donation towards the upkeep of the hounds, inclusion into this elite band of hunters was granted.

So, on a cold morning in mid November, George proudly walked his steed from the stable at the back of the house, and, seeing that she was safe and sound inside the loose box he'd purchased, set off to join the rest of his new playmates at the traditional partaking of a glass of sherry outside The Bowlers Arms.

The horn blew, the dogs cried in unison, the crowd who'd gather to watch this spectacle shouted their words of encouragement. Poor old Bunty buckled under George and went to that green pasture in the sky, leaving the new member without a means of transport and a number of cuts and bruises caused by the tumble into The Bowlers' rose bed.

The vet was called but, after a brief examination, only confirmed what everyone else suspected. Bunty had dropped dead from a mixture of old age, over-excitement, and an enlarged heart caused from years of being over-worked at the fairground riding attraction, where she'd been made to toil from nine in the morning till ten at night, seven days a week. She was fed very little food, given not much love and attention, and an owner that cared more for the beer money she earned him than he ever cared for Bunty.

George never replaced the mare; instead he took her home and gave her a proper burial within the grounds, marking her grave with a fine-cut headstone depicting a graceful galloping steed and the inscription, BUNTY, WHO DIED IN ACTION. Although he wouldn't admit it, he secretly shed a tear or two over the animal which, although he'd only known a short time, he'd become extremely fond of. For had he known about her health from the start, he probably would still have bought her, because of the way she'd gently nuzzled him when they'd first met. Bunty had lived a degrading life, but in death she'd gone with dignity, and George had turned her final resting-place into a shrine.

Needless to say, George's horseback hunting

days were at an end, so instead he turned his attention to shooting, splashing out on the most expensive double barrelled twelve bore shotgun that money could buy, and an automatic clay pigeon skeet, so he could practise at home in his back field. Unfortunately for George, this bordered Gus Devenport's field, enabling him to shoot one of Gus's cows dead with a rather low shot that failed to recognize it had missed its target, and dropped out of the sky right on the border of the two men's land.

George made good the error with a large cheque and a promise to a rather happy Gus, who'd been paid about twice the value of the animal, that he'd be more careful in future. So trying out different directions to do his practising, he managed to shoot the top off a chimney, and destroy a good proportion of the glass in the greenhouse.

Once George felt he was competent enough, he made noises at Warmington Grange about the possibility of taking part in a real live pheasant shoot. But it wasn't from the expected source that the invitation came; instead, it was his old mate Tony Rowlands, supplier of all his lorries' tyres, and drinking partner at the Crown in Chesham.

Tony had been shooting for years, and although he didn't belong to the same social circles as his many hosts, he'd worked his way through the gun club to become captain of the county shooting team; an honour bestowed upon him for the fact that he was the best shot, and not because of who he was.

Although he was from the same background as George, born in the same street, went to the same school, fought in the same gang, Tony was not quite as rough a diamond as the haulage giant.

When it came to putting on the charm, Tony could hold his own with anyone. In fact, the women adored him; so much so, it wasn't unusual to see his Jaguar car making its way up one of the local toff's driveways to indulge in high tea with the mistress of the house while her husband was away on some business trip somewhere.

George told Tony that he wouldn't mind a go at trying his skill at something a little more in keeping with his new-found status rather than a piece of baked clay. So Tony, who had been invited to a shoot at Barnsford Hall the following weekend, told his mate that he would see if he could get him an invite.

Two days later, just as George was heading out to the back field for a spot more practise, the phone rang.

"Hello George, Tony here. Just ringing to let you know that everything's on for the weekend, so I'll pick you up about eight in the morning."

"Cheers, Tony," and with a few more words of casual conversation, George placed the receiver back on the holder and went out with renewed enthusiasm to try and improve his aim.

George, although not unused to early rises, was

up at six o'clock with a vigour that depicted a youngster on Christmas morning. With a quick wash and a shave he was downstairs in his full shooting attire, sitting at the breakfast table and waiting for his breakfast before Mavis had even had time to get her dressing gown on.

At ten minutes to eight he was trampling the gravel at the front of the house, gun in its holder and slung over his shoulder as if he were about to embark on a tiger hunt.

Just as he was examining the time with the aid of his expensive Rolex watch for the tenth time since leaving the house, Tony's Jaguar entered the already-opened gates and made its way up the drive, all the while being followed by the excited wide-eyed gaze of the expectant passenger.

"Morning, George. Sorry I'm late."

"Oh, that's alrit lad. I've not long bin up me sen," George replied nonchalantly, trying to hide the tremble of fervour in his voice as he made himself comfortable in the leather-covered seats of his chum's motor.

"In fact, I nearly rang thee t' say I didner feel up t' going," he continued, hoping his buddy wouldn't detect the lie as he tried the best he could to calm himself down from the prospect of a day's shooting, with what he considered to be the county's finest; and that didn't just mean sharp shooters.

There would be the Squire for a start. George had only met him on one previous occasion, and that was years ago. It was when he'd first started out on his own, and he'd had to go to the hall to complain about a payment that hadn't been fulfilled. Although the Squire apologized, and tried to fob George off with the excuse that it had been an oversight, the two had not actually parted as mutual admirers of one another, something George intended to rectify this time.

Major Bantam occasionally attended these do's, and although George was familiar with the Major, having tried to hold his own with him in conversation at The Bowlers, the sheer demeanour of the man was totally alien to everything George had been brought up to identify, which always left George with an inferiority complex whenever they parted company, but with the determination to do better next time their paths crossed.

The Reverend Bunting sometimes took part in these sporting occasions; that was, if his ministerial duties permitted; and although George had attended church only once (hoping that through the power of prayer he could be elevated to a higher plane within the circles he now moved), he hadn't actually got off on the right foot with the man of the cloth, after he'd remarked to the minister in his usual blunt way, on leaving the church, that he'd have enjoyed the service more if there had been more singing and a lot less talk.

He was sure that none of these issues would be an obstacle in his quest for acceptance amongst the ranks of the aristocracy, and as the journey to the

Barnsford estate came to a juddering conclusion when the Jaguar rattled over the cattle grid and past the lodge of the main entrance, George realised that the whole of his life had been working up to this moment. It was destiny. He'd just been unfortunate to have had the wrong parents. Now all would be put right, as he was about to claim what was rightfully his, (what he'd been reaching out for since the day his mother had looked so disapprovingly at him on receiving the results of his eleven plus); status, and all the trimmings that went with it.

In his mind's eye George could visualize the future. First it would be the OBE or MBE; then in time, when it was right to do so, Sir George Rigby, or Lord Rigby, where he would be able to take his place in the House of Lords and pass judgement on things he knew nothing about, or become a member of an Old Boys' Club, allowing him to commute back and forth from London to Chesham on the train. Pin-striped suit, briefcase, umbrella, his mind raced, until the car pulled up outside the hall and one of the Squire's servants opened the door of the vehicle and let him out.

Soon there were twenty or so men, armed with guns, belts carrying cartridges wrapped around their torsos, dogs running about their feet, and looking as though they were ready to do battle with a tribe of restless natives.

The Squire came out of the Hall, and began organizing the party into the various Land Rovers which were ticking over on the gravelled drive.

George found himself in the company of Lord Brampton, Ziggy Downley, and Captain Josh Twinning, all jolly good friends of the Squire, but not one of them with two brass farthings to rub together. Still, that didn't deter them from bragging about their various dealings, and, how with a bit of backing from the right source, they would all be in clover by this time next year.

George took all this in as he sat bumping up and down on the hard surface of the Land Rover seating, and not realizing that all this talk of financial backing was for his benefit, visualized yet another way of winning his place amongst the gentility.

Arriving at the first shoot, everyone disembarked and gathered around the Squire who was organizing the draw for pegs, which were their positions in a straight line from where the birds would fly. This, by the luck of the draw, would give the lucky ones nearer the front the better chance of bringing a bird down than those towards the back.

Because this was George's first shoot on the Barnsford estate, according to custom, he was allowed to stand at the first peg, which, having weighed the man up, didn't unduly worry the others, as they didn't think he looked as though he could hit a barn door with a cannon.

Squire Barnsford came over to George before the beaters began their noisy clattering through the undergrowth of the little coppice which contained the quarry, and explained the fundamental rules of pheasant shooting.

"Wh-e-n the birds come f-f-f-flying out of th-h-e wood, only shoot f-from the r-r-ight t-to the middle of your b-b-body, d-do not, I r-repeat, d-o-o not fire towards your left. Once t-the bird h-has gone passed you, i-it is the target of the n-n-next in line."

Hoping that he wouldn't have to repeat himself and waste anymore time, he looked at George as if to inquire that everything was understood, to which George nodded his approval, and went to stand at his own peg, four away from George, then gave the orders for the game keeper to start the proceedings.

The setting was perfect. The little wood lay at the bottom of a steep rise, so the birds would have to fly out of the cover and then ascend gradually past the waiting shooting party who stood at their allotted pegs, a distance of about ten yards apart, all the way up the slope.

It meant that no matter how quickly the bird tried to rise, it was never really much higher than shoulder height, as it went flapping with trepidation past the waiting onslaught.

The first bird went by so quickly, George didn't even have time to let off a shot, and was brought down by the Squire himself, where, almost out of respect for their host, there were only a couple of other retorts to be heard.

The second, George remembered pulling the trigger, but by the time he'd come to his senses, the bird was being retrieved by Ziggy Downley's black Labrador retriever.

George was determined he was going to do better with the next one, and, gripping the gun as though he were trying to choke it, he peered down the barrel with bulging eyes as the third bird made a dart away from its cover in search of safety from the advancing beaters.

George couldn't remember any more; he just recalls following the bird with the end of his gun until he'd calmed himself down enough to pull the trigger. 'BANG, BANG.' Both barrels were emptied as George's shoulder jerked back from the retort.

As was always the case when George fired, just before the explosion he closed his eyes tight in anticipation of the noise. When he opened them again a few seconds later, it was to see people running down the hill towards a prostrate Willy Brookhurst, who had occupied the next peg up the line from George.

"Good God, he's hit!" came the cry from Major Bantam, the first to reach the wounded man.

"He's bloody well murdered him," shouted another.

Who, George couldn't make out, but the insinuation that he was a cold-blooded killer, caused him to break into a cold sweat, whereby the gun slipped from his grasp and fell to the ground with a thump.

As the ambulance pulled away with the injured, but still very much alive, Willy Brookhurst, still swearing and shouting and threatening that if he ever gained the use of his right arm again, he'd come looking for the stupid bastard, meaning George. The Squire took Tony Rowlands to one side, and as they observed everyone leering in the direction of George, the Squire recommended that it would be in everyone's favour if Tony took his friend home for his own safety.

And walking back towards the surviving members of his guests, the Squire glanced back and dismissed Tony with, "Oh, a-a-and d-d-don't bring the st-st-stupid prick here again, will you? T-t-that's a good f-fellow."

George never did make it with the county set, which didn't really matter. For three years later he tired of the peace and tranquillity and sold up and moved to Spain, making a vast amount of profit on the property. This allowed him to buy a large villa on the Costa Del Sol, where he found his true persona, becoming friendly and being accepted into the ranks of fellow Brits who'd had no choice in their decision to leave the home country behind, not if they wanted to keep their freedom. Even so, George found them more obliging and thoroughly more hospitable towards him than he'd ever encountered with the nobility. So, exchanging his brogues, plus fours, and tweed jacket for sneakers, Bermuda shorts and flowery shirts, George and

Mavis lived out the rest of their days sipping pina-coladas with their new-found friends from the underworld.

Miss Parkinson stood for a while in the doorway to the newsagent's and pondered upon the meaning of the macabre remark.

CHAPTER TWENTY

A GREEN CHRISTMAS

"Good morning, Mr Devenport, beautiful day for the time of year, isn't it?" Miss Parkinson, spinster of the parish, greeted the larger-than-life farmer as they almost bumped into one another, Gus leaving Harry Gittin's shop, Miss Parkinson entering.

"Well, Miss Parkinson," Gus looked at her cautiously, tapping the side of his nose with his podgy forefinger, "you know what thee say?"

"No, Mr Devenport, what's that?"

"A green Christmas means a full graveyard," and with that he bid her "good day" and waddled off down the street in the direction of The Bowlers, leaving the lady, as he always did, confused and perturbed by his observations.

Miss Parkinson stood for a while in the doorway to the newsagent's and pondered upon the meaning of the macabre remark. Maybe he meant that they'd all pay for the, up until then, extremely mild winter later on with bad conditions, or could he have meant that without the frosts to kill off the bugs and viruses, illnesses would take their toll of the population of Barnsford as the winter progressed?

Gus was always popping such pearls of wisdom into the old lady's head, so that she never knew whether he was warning her in advance of some great catastrophe, or just pulling her leg. Nevertheless, it sent a shiver down her spine as she reflected on the fact that she was no spring chicken herself, and she gave a slight self-induced sneeze and dabbed her runny nose with her pretty embroidered handkerchief, as she recalled what he'd told her the last time she developed a cold.

"It inner the cough what carries thee off. It's the coffin they carry thee off in."

Suddenly the day didn't seem so pleasant, and she found herself longing for a good harsh frost, or perhaps even a blizzard.

That was the week before Christmas; now with the holidays only two days away, Elizabeth Parkinson's sniffle had gone from a runny nose, through the shivering with cold and not able to get warm whatever height she built the fire up to, into a fully-fledged fever, causing her sweat-soaked bedding to feel like sheets of ice against her hot and perspiring body.

Although Doctor Killshaw had assured her it was only another nasty cold, and with gallons of liquids to replenish the body's fluids and plenty of rest, she'd be as right as rain in no time, her mind kept wandering back to her encounter with Gus Devenport, convincing herself that it wouldn't be long now before she'd be reunited with her parents in the kingdom of Heaven.

It didn't help when, on his second visit to see her that day, the good doctor informed her that old Bill Watkins had passed on during the morning, and he'd only been poorly for a couple of days.

Bill was seventy-eight, and looked as though he'd been dead for the last ten years. But somehow he'd managed to drag his skeletal frame down to The Bowlers each night at eight o'clock, where he remained until throwing out time. Then, as if by a miracle, he'd make it past the graveyard, and return home to his bed, where he'd remain until ten o'clock the following morning. Each and every morning the folk of Barnsford would wait in anticipation to see if the curtains of his bedroom would be opened to signal he'd made it through another night. It was this curiosity which led to the doctor being called when Bill's curtains were still drawn together at four in the afternoon.

Bill had died peacefully in his sleep from a heart attack, his sixth; but due to Doctor Killshaw failing to mention this to Miss Parkinson, the old lady convinced herself that Gus's prediction was becoming a reality, and this did nothing to aid her recovery.

It was Christmas Eve when, on leaving his patient marginally recovered, the Doctor happened to mention (just before shutting the front door of the cottage behind him and wishing her a Merry Christmas), that a chap that had lived the other side of Barnsford Hall, someone Miss Parkinson hadn't heard of before, had gone to meet his maker, and that he hoped the funerals wouldn't interfere too much with the season's festivities.

The latest victim of Gus's voodoo had been run over by a cattle wagon while staggering back drunk from The Red Lion at Tilsbury. Although, as a wife beater and a blackguard, he wouldn't be all that sadly missed within the community, it didn't stop the spinster from this time praying beside her bed for the man's soul and a good sharp frost.

By Boxing Day Miss Parkinson was feeling a great deal better, and although she'd only picked at the turkey dinner that had been kindly brought round on Christmas morning by Mrs Crow, her neighbour, she was now feeling her appetite returning with a vengeance. So much so, that the day after Boxing Day she made her way through the warm sunshine to Arthur Blake's grocery shop to restock on provisions.

She'd completely forgotten about the Grim Reaper's presence in the Parish, where, as she wandered through the village, the sunlight flickering on the pond, where the ducks splashing about in the water caused the reflection of the houses to wobble like jellies, she contemplated how lucky she was to be living in such a wonderful place.

"Morning, Miss Parkinson. Shame about poor old Tom Warburton," the grocer greeted her as she entered his shop.

"Why?" the old girl asked. Suddenly remembering the two other deaths, and the fat farmer's prediction.

"Died last night. Haven't heard what from yet, just that his sister came to visit him this morning and found 'im sat upright in 'is chair."

Tom Warburton was the oldest man in the village. Ninety-four, and although he lived in pretty primitive conditions with no running water or electricity (this due to the fact that he refused to let the Squire do any modifications in case the rent went up), he'd always seemed a very healthy man for his age. Doctor Killshaw had consoled Bill's sister with the fact that the old man had not suffered.

"His clock had finally run down," he told her; but Miss Parkinson had now convinced herself that Gus had not only foretold what was happening, but, although unintentionally, had in fact put a curse on the village, which was now unleashing its wrath upon the unsuspecting citizens.

The fourth death came two days later, when Mrs Jeffreys, again in her twilight years, dropped down dead from a severe coronary, more than likely brought on by too many fried breakfasts, dinners and evening meals. The Doctor had been warning her for years about cutting down on her cholesterol, and this before dieticians had been let loose on the masses.

With her puffed-up legs, her three or four chins, and a frame that could eclipse the sun, Joan

Jeffreys could be seen on most days making her way back from the shops, bags laden with supplies, all of which would end up in the frying pan. Even so, with her love for the fatty things in life being the reason given for her demise, she'd still managed to make it to seventy-four, and had never spent a day in bed in her life. So once more Miss Parkinson suspected that the spectre of a green Christmas had struck again.

No one else died that winter; well, not in Barnsford they didn't; instead, over the next three weeks or so, four pregnancies were confirmed.

The first was over three months gone by the time it became public, due to the fact that the mother-to-be was not of marital status and the father had not been confirmed.

It was a wet drizzly day in early summer when, while putting up her brolly as she waited for the nine o'clock bus to Chesham, Miss Parkinson perchanced upon Gus as he made his way down the road to inspect some heifers he had in his lower field.

"Good Morning, Mr Devenport," she greeted the farmer. "What an awful day for the beginning of summer."

To which Gus shook his head with melancholy, and once more tapped the side of his bright red nose with his sausage-like forefinger.

"Rain clouds in June, death's blossoms bloom," and with that he once more bid her "good day" and carried on his journey.

She didn't know whether these were real country sayings, or if Gus just made them up, nevertheless Miss Parkinson put the remark to the back of her mind as the bus pulled up, and paying her fare, she moved to the rear of the coach, where she took possession of her seat and prepared to enjoy her trip into town. It was there she hoped to buy a present for baby Gillian, Mary Lewis's little girl, the first of Barnsford's new generation.